W9-AOD-232

SUPER SCHNOZ

and the

BOOGER BLASTER BREAKDOWN

GARY UREY

pictures by **keith frawley**

ALBERT WHITMAN & COMPANY
CHICAGO, ILLINOIS

Library of Congress Cataloging-in-Publication data is on file with the publisher.

Text copyright © 2015 Gary Urey
Pictures by Keith Frawley
Published in 2015 by Albert Whitman & Company
ISBN 978-0-8075-7562-8

Printed in the United States of America
10 9 8 7 6 5 4 3 2 1 LB 20 19 18 17 16 15

Cover design by Jordan Kost

For more information about Albert Whitman & Company,
visit our web site at www.albertwhitman.com.

For Steve Casino—**G.U.**

Big honking thanks to Michelle, Genevieve, Rachel, and Kaelin. Without you, life would STINK!—**K.F.**

STRANGE SCENT

"Schnoz, what's that weird smell?" Jimmy asked me one day while TJ, Mumps, Vivian, and I were cruising on our bikes down Main Street.

I flared my nostrils and inhaled the luscious, intoxicating scent. My nose hairs tingled with joy, my olfactory bulbs throbbing with delight. The wonderful smell had been wafting in the crisp autumn air of Denmark, New Hampshire, for weeks, and my nose could barely contain its excitement.

"That smell isn't weird," I answered. "It's Strange, as in Jean Paul Puanteur's Strange."

"Huh?" TJ grunted.

"Strange is the name of an extremely popular unisex perfume," Vivian said, steering her bike toward Dr. Wackjöb's Gecko Glue® and Snore Cure Mist® factory. "Every teenager and adult in town wears it."

"Schnoz, let me give you a piece of advice," Jimmy razzed. "Don't let the other guys in school know you like perfume. It could be seriously bad for your honker health."

TJ laughed. "Perfume's for girls."

"Don't tell that to my dad," Mumps said. "He's been spraying himself with Strange every morning for a month."

"Like Vivian said, the perfume is unisex," I replied.

"What's 'unisex' mean?" Jimmy asked.

I hit the brakes, and my bike skidded to a stop. "It means the perfume is suitable for both sexes, male and female."

"My mom loves it too," Vivian added. "She goes through a bottle every two weeks."

"Jean Paul Puanteur is the greatest perfumer

in the world!" I proclaimed. "He's the Mozart of odor, the Picasso of aroma—"

Before I could finish, one of Dr. Wackjöb's delivery trucks whizzed past us. His Gecko Glue® and Snore Cure Mist® products were selling like hotcakes around the world. In fact, they were so successful that *Filthy Rich Review* had featured the company on the cover of its October issue. But the best thing about the business was that it employed hundreds of local people. My mom even got a job there as a quality control supervisor.

"I don't care what anyone thinks," I said to Jimmy after the truck had turned the corner. "I'm not just a one-sniff pony who only likes the smells of dog poop, armpits, and rotting roadkill. I'm a connoisseur of the sweeter scents in life too, you know."

"The art of mixing herb oil, spices, and tree resins to make different fragrances goes all the way back to ancient Babylon," Vivian said. "Perfuming is as old as civilization itself."

TJ rolled his eyes. "Ancient or not, I still say perfume is for girls."

"Stop being a sexist!" Vivian yelled and then held up her fists. "Do you want a bop on the chin?"

"I'm not six!" TJ fired back. "I turned eleven two months ago."

"I said you were a *sexist*, dork butt. A person who stereotypes people based on their gender."

"She's right, TJ," I said. "Apologize. Vivian's smarter and tougher than all of you Not-Right Brothers put together."

TJ kicked a rock with his sneaker. "I'm sorry, but I didn't mean anything by it. I just assumed only girls wore perfume, that's all."

"Well, now you know different," Vivian said. "Let's hurry up and get to Dr. Wackjöb's office. I'm starving."

Every Wednesday, students were released early from school so the teachers could have meetings. We got out at noon and, weather permitting, rode our bikes to Dr. Wackjöb's office for lunch. As we made our way down the street toward the factory, I deeply inhaled the overpowering smell of Strange. Distinguishing among the perfume's different ingredients proved difficult at first, but soon my powerful olfactory receptors downloaded the parts directly into my mental scent dictionary. The perfume's base was ethyl alcohol and distilled water—typical for most perfumes. Next, I sniffed a tantalizing blend of essential oils like lavender, jasmine, sandalwood, and bergamot. I could tell the perfume was of the highest quality because all the ingredients were natural, not one synthetic fragrance in the mix.

The security guard opened the factory gates, and we rolled into the parking lot. I leaned my bike on the rack and took one step toward the office door, and that's when I sensed another extremely subtle, barely detectable ingredient in the Strange concoction. The odor stopped me in my tracks. My nose lifted into the air, huffing like a crazed bloodhound at the scent particles floating on the wind.

"What's wrong, Schnoz?" Vivian asked. "You look like you just smelled a ghost."

"I smell something, all right," I said, my heart thumping. "And I have no idea what it is."

"But you know practically every smell on earth," Mumps said.

I scanned my mental scent dictionary front to back, starting with the pungent odor of a crushed ant and ending with the cheesy aroma of baked ziti. There was nothing, not one tiny whiff of the Strange scent.

FRENCH JASMINE

D<small>r.</small> Wackjöb was chatting on the phone when his secretary escorted us into his office. The overwhelming stench of fresh hákarl blasted up my nostrils. I loved the smell of fermented, urine-soaked shark meat, but the Icelandic delicacy made Vivian and the Not-Right Brothers nearly gag.

Jimmy pulled his T-shirt up over his nose. "Why does Dr. Wackjöb have to eat that disgusting hákarl every single day for lunch?"

"I don't like the smell either," Vivian said. "But we have to give the guy a break. The doctor was a laughingstock in his native Iceland and had to flee. Hákarl reminds him of home."

"Hákarl reminds me of an unflushed toilet," Mumps said with grimace.

"So nice to hear from you, Pierre, and I hope to speak with you soon." Dr. Wackjöb said and then hung up the phone. He pointed to three large pizza boxes sitting on a conference table. "One is plain, one is pepperoni, and the other is black olives and mushrooms. Please, help yourselves."

Vivian, the Not-Brothers, and I tore into the pizzas like starving rescue dogs. Dr. Wackjöb tied a bib around his neck and popped slices of hákarl into his mouth. He chewed very slowly, savoring every shark-pee-flavored bite.

While the gang munched away, my nose drifted off to the mysterious smell locked inside Strange. The fragrance resembled vanilla, but the unknown aroma was way more earthy, funky, and bold than any variety I had ever come across during my scent-gathering expeditions. Only a master like Jean Paul Puanteur could confuse my world-class sniffer like this!

8

Most kids my age have posters of actors, musicians, and athletes hanging on their bedroom walls. As for me, I have only a small, eight-by-ten framed picture of Jean Paul Puanteur. I clipped the photo from a *National Geographic* magazine article about the art and science of making perfume. He is standing in a field of extremely rare and expensive French jasmine, wearing a black tuxedo with bright red Converse sneakers, a brilliant orange sun high in the sky. The man is a scent artist of the highest order.

A set of greasy fingers snapped in front of my face.

"Earth to Schnoz," Vivian said, ripping me out of my French jasmine daze. "You're staring blankly into space. What are you thinking about?"

"Strange," I said.

TJ fanned the air in front of his face. "I wish I had a bottle of Strange right now. I'd spray it around the room to get rid of the hákarl stink!"

Dr. Wackjöb laughed. "Iceland's secret shark recipe goes all the way back to the time of Vikings. What is this Strange you speak of?"

"Strange is a ridiculously popular perfume," Mumps answered. "Everybody's wearing the stuff."

"I'm a huge fan of the perfuming arts," I said. "But there's one ingredient in Strange that my snuffer can't sniff out."

Dr. Wackjöb raised his white, bushy eyebrows. "You, the one and only Super Schnoz, cannot recognize a scent? I don't believe it. Your nose is to smells what Einstein's brain was to physics."

"Well, this is one odor equation I have yet to crack."

"I don't know anything about the perfume business," Dr. Wackjöb continued. "But just as my company has a secret ingredient—synthetic setae developed from the sticky pads on a gecko's feet—I would assume perfumers use secret ingredients as well."

I shrugged. "You're probably right, but if I don't figure out that smell and add it to my scent dictionary I'm going to blow a booger!"

"Perhaps I should call back Pierre and ask him."

"Who's Pierre?" Vivian asked.

"He's the gentleman I was talking to on the

phone as you arrived for lunch. He's a Frenchman, an old friend of mine from when I studied geology for a year at the University Lille Nord de France. I hadn't spoken with him in thirty years. He phoned me out of blue after reading about my successful business in *Filthy Rich Review*."

"Why would this Pierre person know about secret ingredients found in perfume?" I asked.

"Gríðarstór Nef, my old friend's full name is Pierre du Voleur, owner of the Français Scent Company, makers of fine perfumes and fragrances."

I sat up in my seat, nose hairs quivering with excitement. "Can you ask him about the mystery ingredient in Strange?"

"That won't do any good," Vivian said.

"Why?"

"Strange is made by Jean Paul Puanteur, a completely different company. Coke would never give up its secret soda formula to Pepsi. Why would two rival perfume companies share ingredients?"

"She's right, Schnoz," Jimmy said. "If you want to figure out that smell, you'll have to huff it out for yourself."

The scent receptors inside my honker deflated a little. The task would be daunting, but I had never met a smell my nose couldn't defeat, and Strange was not going to provide the first.

ODOR-BLINDNESS

The mysterious odor molecules inside Strange teased my nose during the day and haunted my dreams at night. How could I not know what that last scent is? For the next week, I put myself through a vigorous set of smell exercises. Just as a bodybuilder pumps heavy weights to make their muscles grow, I attempted to expand my olfactory senses by immersing myself with the smelliest things in town.

I spent a hot and humid Saturday locked inside the overflowing port-o-potty at the high school football field. The overwhelming reek of liquefied poop, sopping toilet paper, and stale urine made my eyes water and nose hairs curl. After that, I shoved one of my dad's rancid running shoes over my nose and mouth like a surgical mask. The foot fungus rot penetrated my nasal cavity and absorbed into my sinuses. I then took a midnight dip in the wastewater treatment pond.

Other than an extremely itchy red rash, I got nothing from the sewer plant splash or any of my other odor-immersion experiments. My smelling

confidence sunk to an all-time low. The secret scent of Strange was slipping further away from my dictionary of scents.

"Have you figured out the Strange smell yet?" Mumps asked me one afternoon when Vivian, the Not-Right Brothers, and I were hanging out in our top-secret hideaway, the Nostril.

"No," I said. "And I don't feel like talking about it."

"But you're a smelling prodigy!" Jimmy proclaimed. "Your superhuman snoot is capable of detecting over a trillion scents."

"This reminds me of when the Thing spontaneously reverted back to human form and lost all of his Thing powers." Mumps said.

"I'm not losing my superpowers!" I growled. "I defeated greedy polluters and a giant nose rocket from outer space that was intent on destroying Earth!"

Vivian grabbed my nostrils and forced me into a chair. "Schnoz, settle down before you blow a snot bubble. We know this Strange aroma has been tough on you. Let's all put our noses together and think of what to do."

I let out a frustrated sigh. "I've tried everything. The smell in Strange resembles some kind of spicy vanilla, but it's nothing my sniffer has ever encountered before."

"Well, there's one good thing about the smell," Jimmy said.

"What's that?" I asked.

"It doesn't stink. In fact, the smell is kind of nice."

"This isn't about whether the smell is good or bad," Vivian said. "The odor is personal for Schnoz. Smelling is his whole identity. Just imagine if you suddenly couldn't smell your favorite foods like pizza, hamburgers, or—"

"Or bean burritos!" Mumps interjected. "Mexican food is my favorite even though it gives me really stinky gas."

"TMI—too much information," Vivian said, rolling her eyes.

TJ, who had been silent the whole time, looked up from his laptop. "Schnoz may have anosmia."

"Huh?" I grunted.

"While you four were bickering," TJ continued,

"I've been researching and have come across a medical condition called anosmia."

"I don't have insomnia," I said. "Since the aliens stopped harvesting my snores, I sleep like a puppy at night."

"A-nos-mi-a," TJ pronounced slowly, accenting each syllable. "Not insomnia."

"What's anosmia?" Vivian asked.

"It's a medical condition sometimes referred to as odor-blindness."

"I don't even know what odor-blindness means," I blurted out.

"When someone can't tell one color from another, it is called being color-blind," TJ explained. "Anosmia is the same thing only with smells."

"What's the cause?" Mumps asked.

TJ clicked a link on the anosmia web page and started reading. "'Anosmia can be caused by a severe inflammation of the nasal passages due to allergies or a cold virus; severe blows to the head causing a concussion or head trauma; deviated nasal septum or crooked nose; nasal polyps; tumors; different medications,' and a hundred other reasons."

My heart sunk into my chest. I felt the blood drain from my face. The room started spinning; my breath came in quick huffs. Tears formed in my eyeballs, but I didn't want Vivian or the Not-Right Brothers to see me cry. This was the moment I had been dreading since discovering my proboscis powers. At one time or another, every superhero—Spider-Man, Superman, the Invisible Woman, Green Lantern, Human Torch, Wolverine, and dozens of others—lost all of their super powers.

"Without my supersized snort detector, I'm just a mortal kid with a big nose ripe for ridicule," I said with a shaky voice. "Everybody at school will start picking on me again."

"Nobody will pick on you," Jimmy said and then held up his fist. "If any kid makes fun of your nose, I'll give them my five-fingered sandwich."

Vivian gently patted the bridge of my nose. "Just because you can't detect one single ingredient inside a bottle of perfume doesn't mean you have a smell disorder," she said. "There has to be an anosmia test you can take."

"There is such a test," TJ said. "A company called Sniffsonics sells a product called OINK—the Odor Identification Nasal Kit. It's self-administered and perfect for people who think they may have anosmia."

"Then order the kit," Mumps said. "How much is it?'

"We can get one for the bargain price of four hundred and ninety-nine dollars and ninety-nine cents, plus shipping and handling."

"Ugh!" I groaned. "We don't have that kind of money."

"*We* don't have that much money," Vivian said. "But we know someone who does."

"Who?" TJ asked.

Vivian slipped on her bicycle helmet. "Come on, guys. We need to take a ride and have a little chat with Dr. Wackjöb."

We all hopped on our bikes and pedaled to the Gecko Glue® and Snore Cure Mist® Factory.

SNIFFING STICKS

"Gríðarstór Nef needs four hundred and ninety-nine dollars and ninety-nine cents for what kind of test?" Dr. Wackjöb asked after we burst into his office.

"Plus shipping and handling," Mumps chimed in.

"Anosmia," Vivian said. "Some people call it odor-blindness."

Dr. Wackjöb stared long and hard at my honker. "Are you having some kind of smell difficulties?"

"Yes!" I exclaimed. "It happened for the first time when we were all standing in this very room. Don't you remember—the secret ingredient in

Strange? I can detect over a trillion smells, but that single, vanilla-like odor is leaving my snot maker high and dry."

"We're afraid Schnoz might have a scent disorder," TJ said. "We have to buy a test called the Odor Identification Nasal Kit. Sniffsonics is the only company in the world that sells it."

A look of worry washed over Dr. Wackjöb's face. "My friend, your snuffler is not only a gift from the heavens above, but an American treasure. We must do everything possible to keep it in proper working order." He grabbed a pen and wrote a check for the entire amount.

* * *

The kit arrived in the mail a week later. Vivian, the Not-Right Brothers, and I gathered inside the Nostril and opened the box.

"I can't believe this thing was so expensive." Jimmy groaned. "It's just an instruction booklet, a blindfold, and a bunch of fancy-looking markers."

"Those aren't markers," Vivian said as she skimmed through the instructions. "They're called sniffing sticks."

"What's a sniffing stick?" Mumps asked.

I reached out to grab one of them, but Vivian cuffed the tip of my nose.

"Stay away, Schnoz," she said. "These sniffing sticks are the main component of your smell test."

"Excuse me, Miss Know-It-All," I said sarcastically. "Then why don't you explain how this whole thing works?"

Vivian held up a DVD that came with kit. "Let's watch this first."

TJ popped the DVD into his laptop. The narrator was an old guy who called himself Professor Stickle. He wore a white lab coat and big, round glasses that nearly took up his whole face. We were surprised to learn that Professor Stickle originally designed the Odor Identification Nasal Kit to test members of the armed forces with olfactory-sensitive jobs.

"I'm the test administrator," Vivian said when the DVD was over. "Schnoz, just like Professor Stickle says, we need to find a quiet, odor-free space for testing."

"The Nostril should be fine," Jimmy said.

"The Professor said it must be an odor-free space," Vivian countered. "Your sweaty armpits smell like you just ran a marathon. TJ smells like he just took a bath in a garbage can, and Mumps's breath reeks like he hasn't brushed his teeth in a month."

I nodded my nose. "She's right, guys. You three stink pretty badly, but I kind of like it. In fact, Mumps's breath is so uniquely rancid that I'm going to add it to my scent dictionary."

"Gross," Vivian said with a grimace. "Schnoz, let's ride our bikes to the library and use one of the study rooms."

We loaded the Odor Identification Nasal Kit into Vivian's backpack and then headed to the Denmark Public Library.

The library had three private study rooms, all of which were in use when Vivian and I got there. You could only use the rooms for an hour at a time, so Vivian and I had to wait twenty minutes for one to open up. Vivian killed the time by re-searching anosmia on the Internet. I browsed the comic book section, poring over superhero stories for some guidance about my loss-of-powers problem.

I found some comfort in an issue of Uncanny X-Men when Storm lost her ability to control weather. The government shot her with a weapon specifically designed to neutralize the powers of mutants. She eventually got her powers back by spending a year on a parallel Earth and making a machine that restored her powers. Where could I find a parallel Earth to solve my problem? The only planet outside our solar system that I knew of was Apnea, and those snore suckers wanted to kill me!

"Our room's opening up," Vivian said.

We stepped into the study room and closed the door. The room did not offer complete privacy. Instead of four solid walls, one wall had a big window facing the reference librarian's desk. Anybody walking down the hall could see right inside.

"The librarian can see exactly what we're doing," I said, plopping down at the table.

"So what?" Vivian remarked. "We're not doing anything wrong. Just doing a little smell test, that's all."

Vivian unzipped her backpack and retrieved the Odor Identification Nasal Kit. The contents of the kit included sixteen different sniffing sticks, three sheets of paper with numbered little ovals to fill in like those on a standardized test, and a black blindfold.

"Why do I need a blindfold?" I asked.

"Because that's what the instructions say. Put it on."

I slipped the blindfold over my nose and then around my eyes. Everything instantly turned dark.

"Now, pay careful attention," Vivian instructed. "I'm going to hold a series of three different sniffing sticks up to your nostrils. Two of the sticks are the same smell and one is different—but extremely minutely. All you have to do is take a whiff of each stick and then tell me which one has the different smell. Got it?"

I took a deep breath. "Ready when you are."

"Okay. When you give me an answer, I'll record the results on the data sheet. Here we go. Ready, sniff!"

With a big huff of my honker, the familiar scent

of butanol, the basis for most French fragrances filled my nostrils.

Vivian then held up two more sniffing sticks to my nose.

"Which stick was different from the other?" she asked.

"Easy," I answered. "I detect that Stick Two was not the same."

There was a scribbling sound as Vivian filled in an oval on the data sheet. For the next forty-five minutes, Vivian held up different sniffing sticks to my nose. Each level of smell detection grew more difficult. When I had sniffed the last stick, my nose felt like it had been through a smell-a-thon.

As Vivian compared my responses with the test's answer key, my heart raced like a bunny rabbit at a falconry festival. The consequences were as clear as snot running out of my nose on a bad allergy day—if I'd failed the test, my super sniffing powers were slipping away forever.

"Done," Vivian finally said. "Do you want to hear how you did?"

"Yes!" I cried out so loudly that the reference

librarian pounded on the window and held a finger to her lips.

"A perfect score is one hundred. Schnoz, I'm sorry to inform you that your score was…"

Time stopped; Earth ceased to rotate on its axis. Beads of sweat formed on my temples. My nostrils throbbed like an exposed artery. The next word from Vivian's mouth would determine my entire future.

"One hundred!" Vivian screeched. "You got a perfect score. You don't have odor-blindness. According to this test, your nose is in perfect working order."

The librarian pounded on the window again, signaling us to be quiet, but I didn't care. I raised my nose, sucked in a big nostril full of air, and let out the most joyful trumpet snort ever.

CHAPTER 5

THE BOY WITH A THOUSAND SCENTS

My booger blaster may have been in fine working order, but the secret ingredient in Strange was still unknown. I was beginning to think the smell might be one of the great mysteries of the universe. Like the origins of life or the cheeseburger Mumps keeps in his underwear drawer that still hasn't decomposed after eleven months.

Thankfully, my nose had no problem flying. Whenever I got depressed about Strange, I slipped on my Super Schnoz costume, turned my nostrils into massive hot air balloons, and floated into the clouds. I buzzed over the town of Denmark and into the White Mountain National Forest. The burned-out remnants of Dr. Wackjöb's Center for UFOs, Earthquakes, and Alien Abduction lay below me like a giant scar on the earth. Huge chunks of Apnean metal from when I blew up Robo-Nose littered the grounds. In less than a year, my nose had defeated an evil environmental company intent on destroying our town and saved the Earth from alien domination. Yet, one barely noticeable ingredient in a bottle of perfume was stopping my sniffer cold.

I was about to land and walk around the ruins of the compound when a familiar smell wafted into my nostrils. The scent was from an aerosol can of novelty fart spray. Just like the Gotham City Police Department uses the Bat Signal to summon Batman, the Not-Right Brothers and Vivian use the fart spray to contact me. I closed one nostril, banked sharply to the left, and flew as fast as I could to our secret hideout.

Dr. Wackjöb and the gang were waiting for me when I got there.

"We're going to New York City!" Jimmy exclaimed.

"What are you talking about?" I asked.

"New York City, baby!" Mumps hollered, spewing more fart spray into the air.

Vivian fanned the rancid air away from her face. "Knock it off with the fart spray already. Schnoz is present and accounted for."

"I've never been to New York before," TJ added.

"Time out," I said. "What's all this about going to New York?"

"Remember my old friend, Pierre du Voleur?" Dr. Wackjöb asked me.

"Sure. He's the guy who owns the Français Scent Company. What about him?"

"We spoke again this morning. I told him about your impressive olfactory skills, and he wants to meet you. He found tales of your proboscis power very intriguing. Especially your extensive mental scent dictionary."

My eyes lit up and my nostrils flared. "For real? An international French perfumer wants to meet me?"

"Absolutely," Dr. Wackjöb said. "After I entertained him with tales of your sniffing adventures, he said, 'I must meet *le garçon aux mille parfums.*'"

"What does that mean?" Vivian asked.

"It means 'the boy with a thousand scents' in French," Dr. Wackjöb answered.

"More like the boy with a *trillion* scents," TJ chimed in.

The news was overwhelming. A real person in the perfume industry wanted to meet me. Even though I didn't know a thing about Pierre du Voleur or the Français Scent Company, the fact that a living, breathing creator of perfumes knew about my nose was an incredible honor.

"Why do we have to meet him in New York?" I asked. "Why can't he come to see us here?"

Dr. Wackjöb smiled. "That is the best part! Pierre explained that an art show devoted exclusively to scent is opening in New York the week of October 12. The show is called the Art of Odor, the world's first major museum exhibit devoted exclusively to recognizing scent as a major medium of artistic expression."

"I know all about!" I exclaimed. "I've been reading about the show online. It's going to focus on fifteen major perfumers and twelve works, including Jean Paul Puanteur. I'll finally be able to meet the Mozart of odor, the Picasso of aroma, and ask him about the secret of Strange!

"Our weeklong school break is from October 12 to 16," Vivian said. "Maybe we can go!"

"Count me and my nose in," I gushed. "This is like a dream come true!"

"When do we leave?" TJ asked.

"This coming Monday morning," Dr. Wackjöb answered. "We will be staying in New York for an entire week."

"I doubt my parents will allow me to go for that long," Vivian said.

"Mine too," Mumps added.

"No need to worry, children," Dr. Wackjöb reassured us. "I have already spoken to each of your parents. This will be a weeklong educational field trip to the most exciting city in the world. They were all very comfortable with me being your adult chaperone."

Vivian and the Not-Right Brothers let out an enthusiastic cheer. TJ fired up his laptop and researched New York City tourist sites. The gang gathered around him, super-excited about all the places they would visit. Seeing Central Park and climbing to the top of the Empire State Building would be fun, but for me the week was more than just a field trip. I would finally rub noses with people obsessed with scents, just like me.

"Start packing," Dr. Wackjöb advised. "I'm going to arrange our airline flights and hotel accommodations."

"Go ahead and reserve our rooms," I said, "but don't worry about buying airline tickets."

"Driving a car or taking the train will take way too long," Dr. Wackjöb said.

I dragged out the harness I had used to fly everybody into the White Mountain National Forest when I battled the Apneans and booger blobs. Jimmy's artful stitchwork on the fabric was still perfect, right down to the feathers that made me look like a pregnant turkey buzzard.

"What are you doing with that thing?" Mumps asked.

"We're not taking an airplane to New York City," I said. "I'm flying us all there with my nose."

UP, UP, AND AWAY!

"Where's Dr. Wackjöb?" Jimmy wondered, looking at his watch. "We all agreed to meet in front of the Nostril at six forty-five a.m. sharp. He's already ten minutes late."

Everyone milled around Jimmy's backyard, anxious for our trip to New York. Mumps carried a big Denmark High School duffel bag. TJ and Jimmy lugged two overstuffed backpacks, and Vivian carted two pieces of luggage. She said one was full of clothes and toiletries; the other was what she called her "carry-on" bag, whatever that meant.

I didn't care that Dr. Wackjöb was running late. My main concern was how my nose would get us off the ground with all the extra weight. Launching with just Vivian and the Not-Right Brothers was challenging enough. But I assumed I could carry them plus Dr. Wackjöb. I hadn't thought about the extra weight of the luggage. My flying honker did not come with a standard operating manual, so I had no way of knowing if the harness Jimmy had stitched together could support everyone. Maybe we should have taken the airline after all.

Before expressing my concerns, a big Gecko Glue® and Snore Cure Mist® delivery truck backed into Jimmy's driveway. Dr. Wackjöb and a driver got out of the truck, flipped open the roll-up door, and hoisted out a large wicker basket the size of a car. Luckily, Jimmy's parents were at work so they didn't see what was going on.

"What's that for?" Vivian asked.

"One moment," Dr. Wackjöb answered as he and the driver gently set the wicker basket on the grass.

"That thing looks like a picnic basket for a giant," TJ observed.

"Or for Little Red Riding Hood on steroids," Mumps added.

Dr. Wackjöb waited until the truck pulled out of the driveway and then said, "How do you like our gondola?"

Jimmy scratched his head. "A gondo…what?"

"Gondola," Dr. Wackjöb repeated.

"But a gondola is a boat used on Venetian canals to row tourists around," Vivian said. "My parents rode in one when they stayed at a hotel in Las Vegas."

"That is true, young lady. A gondola can also be the name of a large basket suspended beneath a hot-air balloon."

Vivian, the Not-Right Brothers, and I looked at each other with similar wide-eyed expressions.

"You want Schnoz to use this basket instead of the harness to fly us to New York!" TJ exclaimed.

"I don't know about this," I said. "Carrying all of you, the luggage, plus this huge basket looks a little overwhelming even for my giant flapping nostrils."

"Gríðarstór Nef, if your nose can destroy an alien space ship intent on taking over the earth then it surely can propel us all to New York in a gondola," Dr. Wackjöb said. "I will not travel with all of us smashed together in a canvas sack like a bunch of groceries. This gondola means we soar to New York in comfort and style!"

Vivian and the Not-Right Brothers tossed their luggage into the gondola and then climbed inside. I ran behind the Nostril, stripped off my street clothes, and pulled on my Super Schnoz outfit and Mardi Gras mask.

"I hope we don't have to crash land in some farmer's corn field," I said, still unsure of whether I could carry all the extra weight."

Dr. Wackjöb chuckled as he draped two thick ropes over my shoulders. "You'll be fine, Gríðarstór Nef. I have complete confidence in your nose."

"These ropes feel like Burmese pythons trying to suffocate me," I groaned.

"They need strength and weight to keep us stable during flight," Dr. Wackjöb said. He then attached the opposite ends of the ropes to the gondola and climbed inside with his suitcase.

"Let's get this bad boy in the air," TJ ordered. "I want to be in New York before noon."

The breeze was light at first, but soon a hard gust of wind shot through Jimmy's backyard. I sucked in as much air as humanly possible. My nostrils inflated like a giant bounce house at a kid's birthday party. My toes lifted off the ground, cape fluttering in the breeze. I was hovering in the air, but the gondola didn't budge an inch.

"This thing's too heavy!" I hollered. "I can't lift it off the ground."

"Keep trying!" Vivian shouted to me.

"You can't turn back now," Jimmy added.

"Schnoz! Schnoz! Schnoz!" TJ and Mumps chanted, trying to encourage me.

I inhaled deeper. My nostrils had expanded to their maximum point. If they spread any further, my beak would burst apart and unleash gallons of snot all over my friends. Finally, the gondola ascended a few feet in the air. The sudden lurch caused everyone to fall backward on their butts.

"This thing should have come with seat belts," I heard Mumps complain.

The gondola and I were now engaged in a brutal game of tug-of-war. I was trying to defy Newton's universal law of gravity, and the gondola was fighting to stay on the ground. I sniffed, huffed, and snuffled with all my might. Still, I was losing the battle. There was no way we'd get to New York at this rate.

"Use some of this!" Vivian shouted and then tossed me a jar of cayenne pepper.

"Why?" I asked. "Do you want me to blow something up?"

"Great idea!" TJ exclaimed. "Schnoz, sniff the pepper and turn your snot maker into a rocket!"

"TJ and Vivian are right," Dr. Wackjöb said. "Just as the space shuttle uses a pair of solid rocket boosters and liquid hydrogen to initiate launch, you can use your pair of massive nostrils and cayenne pepper to propel us into the sky."

"You have solid rocket boogers!" Mump screeched.

I quickly opened the jar of pepper, took two big

snorts, and sneezed so hard I thought my nasal lining would hemorrhage. A fiery blast of red-hot mucous shot from my stinging nostrils. The ropes around my shoulders stiffened, and we thrust into the sky like an arrow shot from a bow.

"Up, up, and away!" I cheered as the clouds grew thicker and the town of Denmark disappeared below my feet.

CHAPTER 7

EENEY, MEENY, MINEY, MOE

Once we had reached an altitude of five thousand feet, I stopped sniffing the cayenne pepper and flicked off my solid rocket boogers. I was floating on the swirling breeze in a southwest direction. Every now and then, I looked down to check on the gang. From the smiles on their faces, they were having a great flight.

"There's the Hudson River," I informed them. "We just follow the river south all the way to our destination!"

"How long will it take to get there?" Jimmy asked.

I tilted my nose and gauged the wind speed.

"The wind is gusting at about forty miles per hour," I said. "New York City is sixty miles away. That means we'll be there in ninety minutes."

Everyone hooted their approval as I set my course for the Big Apple.

The rolling fields and thick woods of the countryside soon gave way to civilization. In the distance, the massive skyline of New York City came into view. The sight was both awe inspiring and intimidating. Questions tumbled in my mind. *Where will we land? How will I hide the gondola? Will New Yorkers make fun of my nose?* Before I could think of any more questions, a huge jet airliner whizzed overhead. The massive draft of wind made the gondola wobble in midair like a crazy spinning top.

"I'm going to be sick," I heard Mumps whimper.

I quickly plugged my nostrils, began our descent, and stabilized the gondola. Iconic sights came into view—the Statue of Liberty, the Empire State Building, and a swath of green among the buildings that had to be Central Park.

"Land in the park," TJ said.

As I circled around the park searching for a landing place, a crowd of people standing next to a lake looked up at me.

"Check that thing out." I heard a man say.

"It's some kind of hot-air balloon," said another.

"And the balloon is shaped like a kid with a huge nose!" someone else commented.

Dr. Wackjöb hollered up to me. "Gríðarstór Nef, do not land in the park!"

"Why?" I asked.

"There are eight million people in New York City. We can't risk someone damaging the gondola. You'll have to find another place to set this thing down."

Frustrated, I inflated my nostrils again and floated above the skyline.

"Drop the gondola on top of a skyscraper!" Vivian shouted to me.

"But which one?" I wondered aloud. "There are hundreds of them poking into the clouds."

"Select one with a flat roof," Dr. Wackjöb suggested.

I circled the city like a vulture searching for a dead animal carcass. Twenty blocks south of Central Park, I spied two buildings that looked promising. They were side by side, had flat roofs, and were of medium height. I didn't want the structures to be a zillion stories when we had to walk down a back stairwell to ground level. Finally, I picked one using the trusted *eeney, meeny, miney, moe* method and landed perfectly on the black-tar roof.

"It feels great to be on solid ground again," Jimmy said.

"We're not on solid ground yet," TJ said. "Technically, we are standing on top of hundreds of tons of steel beams and reinforced concrete."

"What's that big round tower?" Mumps asked, pointing to a rusty-looking structure in the far corner of the roof.

"It holds water," Dr. Wackjöb answered. "The city can't supply enough water pressure because the buildings are so tall. They must have their own pumps and water towers."

Vivian yanked open a heavy door. "This is the

way to the street," she said. "Let's check into our hotel and see the sights!"

I changed out of my Super Schnoz costume and joined the gang in the stairwell. The building had twenty stories, so it took us a good fifteen minutes to hike all the way to street level. As soon as my nose hit the sidewalk, dozens of tantalizing smells bombarded my olfactory senses: rotting garbage, onion bagels, stale pee, burning meat from food vendors, hot steam drifting from

street grates, taxi-cab exhaust, pepperoni pizza, soft pretzels, coffee, and…

Strange!

Hundreds of people clogged the busy sidewalks, and most of them were wearing my favorite perfume. The sweet scent wafted off napes of necks, crooks of elbows, and pulsing wrists. I sniffed harder, hoping the barrage of Strange would help me uncover the elusive vanilla-like mystery ingredient. There was nothing. Just a big question mark among the gentle mixes of lavender, jasmine, sandalwood, and bergamot.

"Here's the hotel," Dr. Wackjöb announced.

I looked up and saw a big sign welcoming us to the Lexington Avenue Hotel. The doorwoman loaded our luggage onto a cart, and we stepped inside. The hotel's lobby was small with black marble floors, lots of fake plants, and a massive oak check-in desk. Dr. Wackjöb had reserved four rooms: one for him, one for Vivian, and two others for the Not-Right Brothers and me to share.

"I refuse to sleep in the same room as Mumps," Jimmy said. "He farts in his sleep."

"Then you and TJ share, and I'll bunk with Mumps," I said. "I find his middle-of-the-night explosions oddly endearing."

We rode the elevator to our rooms, unpacked our suitcases, and then all met back down at the lobby. As we were deciding what attraction to see first, the hotel door opened and in walked a scrawny young man wearing a red beret and carrying a white sign that read: *Dr. Wackjöb and Friends*.

"I am Dr. Wackjöb," said Dr. Wackjöb.

"And we're his friends," Vivian added.

"Who are you?" Mumps asked.

"My name is Arnaud," the man said with a thick French accent. "I am Pierre du Voleur's personal assistant and chauffeur. He wants you to meet him at the Museum of Olfactory Art." Arnaud turned his attention to me. "From the looks of your nose, you must be the infamous Andy Whiffler. Monsieur du Voleur is very excited to meet you."

"Call me Schnoz," I said, and then we all hopped into a Hummer stretch limousine and sped up the avenue.

CHAPTER 8

THE ART
OF ODOR

Arnaud steered the Hummer through the busy New York streets. The inside of the vehicle was awesome—cushy leather seats, tinted windows, a mini refrigerator stocked with soda, and two flat-panel TV screens with DVD players.

"The last person to use this limousine was dousing themselves with lots of Strange," I said. "The smell is really strong."

"Do you like Strange, Schnoz?" Arnaud asked, smiling at me through the rearview mirror.

"I love it! Strange smells great, plus Jean Paul Puanteur was the creator. He's the greatest perfumer on the planet."

"Some think Puanteur is the best. Others think Monsieur du Voleur is better."

"I've never smelled any of Pierre du Voleur's perfumes."

"You must be joking," Arnaud said. "Monsieur du Voleur created such classic scents as Snakebite, Love Kills, Secretions, and his most popular, *Bête Blanc*—White Beast."

I shook my nose. "Sorry, I've never heard of them or smelled them."

Arnaud's smile turned into a frown. "Don't worry. The fragrances of Pierre du Voleur will soon rise to the top, and Jean Paul Puanteur will kneel before his greatness."

He then raised the partition window that separated the driver from the passengers. The Hummer raced angrily through a yellow light, barely missing a group of pedestrians. We all stared out the windows in awe as the Empire State Building came into view.

"Sounds like Arnaud doesn't like Jean Paul Puanteur very much," Vivian whispered.

"From what I understand," Dr. Wackjöb said, "there are a lot of cutthroats and much back-stabbing in the perfuming world. The scent artists must closely guard their creations from rival companies who want to steal their ingredients and make knockoffs."

"Kind of like the glue and snore cure business," TJ offered.

Dr. Wackjöb nodded. "You are correct. If the secret of synthetic gecko feet ever got out, I'd be out of business within a year."

The Hummer suddenly screeched to a stop in front of a white building that looked like a giant tower of Jenga blocks. Outside, women wearing fancy evening gowns and men in black tuxedoes hovered around the entrance.

"Why are all those people dressed up?" Mumps asked.

The partition window slowly rolled opened. "Because the opening of a new art exhibit is a chic affair," Arnaud said.

"What's 'sheek' mean?" Mumps asked.

"It means 'classy' in French," Dr. Wackjöb said.

"Give them your name at the doors," Arnaud instructed. "Monsieur du Voleur is expecting you."

The moment I stepped out of the Hummer, all of the elegantly dressed couples stopped what they were doing and stared at my nose. My stomach tangled up like a set of earbud cables. Their reactions to my sniffinator brought back unhappy memories of my first few weeks at James F. Durante Elementary School.

"Ignore them, Schnoz," Vivian said. "Your nose is a gift from the gods, and don't you ever forget it."

Her words made me feel a lot better. These people knew nothing about me or the power of my honker. They had no idea that I had saved the world from snotty aliens and evil polluters. I flung my muzzle in the air, took a confident whiff, and walked into the Museum of Olfactory Art with the rest of the gang.

We gave the ticket person our names and strolled into the exhibit. I had been to the Classic Arcade Museum in Laconia and the Salem Witch Museum in Massachusetts, but the Art of Odor exhibit was something completely different. The smell of perfume was everywhere, floating like invisible scent pods on the still air. We were standing in a large white room with twelve curvy indentations in the walls. I watched people step up to an indentation, take a whiff, and then move on to the next one.

"Go on, Schnoz," Jimmy said. "You have the honor of taking the first sniff."

I took a deep breath and stepped up to the wall. There were two holes at the base of the indentation. As soon as my snuffler got close, a puff of perfume shot from the holes. It was kind of like taking a slurp from a water fountain. A brief description of the perfume flashed on the wall, but I already recognized the fragrance before reading a single sentence.

"Mammal No. 5 by Eugene Mammifère!" I gushed and then quickly moved on to the next smell.

After an exhilarating half hour with my nose pressed against the wall breathing such classics as Sticky by Jacques Gluant, Dracula Noir by Otto Sang, and the incomparable Strange by Jean Paul Puanteur, I was ready for something new.

"Do you know what I find extremely interesting

from reading the history of these perfumes?" Vivian asked.

"What?" I mumbled, still intoxicated by all the beautiful smells.

"Perfumers used only natural scents until the early twentieth century. After that, nearly all of them switched over to synthetic materials."

"But not Jean Paul Puanteur," I said. "He uses only natural ingredients. That's why Strange is so excellent."

We moved from the main gallery to a smaller room with a bunch of different exhibitions. One of them was about how perfumers layered their scents to make one unified smell. TJ and Mumps spent the bulk of their time here, trying to learn how coffee, spearmint Life Savers, garlic bagel with cream cheese, bad breath, and body odor all mixed to give Principal Cyrano such an awful stench.

Vivian, Jimmy, Dr. Wackjöb, and I sat at a long glass table in the middle of the room. Twelve bowls were on the table, each filled with a scent represented in the main gallery. A museum guide encouraged us to dab a wooden stick into one of the bowls, take a sniff, and then go to a computer terminal and log how the scent made us feel.

Only one sentence came to my mind—*I think I died and woke up in aroma heaven!*

As I was about to join TJ and Mumps, Arnaud and another man walked into the room. The man accompanying Arnaud was tall with slicked-back hair and wearing a black tuxedo. A licorice-thin mustache outlined his upper lip.

"Pierre!" Dr. Wackjöb said enthusiastically, shaking the man's hand. "You haven't changed a bit in thirty years!"

The man patted Dr. Wackjöb's balding head. "I wish I could say the same about you, Aðalbjörn."

Both men laughed.

Dr. Wackjöb turned his attention to me. "This is the young man I have told you about. Pierre du Voleur, meet Andy Whiffler, the boy with the most powerful sense of smell on the planet."

I stuck out my hand, but Pierre du Voleur did not offer to shake. He just stared intently at my nose, his gaze like a hungry tiger ready to pounce on an unsuspecting goat.

CHAPTER 9

STRANGE IS AS STRANGE DOES

"*Excusez moi* while I indulge," Pierre du Voleur said with a thick French accent. He then proceeded to invade my personal space by gently spreading open my nostrils with his fingertips, flicking on a penlight, and peering deep inside my sniffer like a doctor examining a patient.

"You have the most *fantastique* olfactory bulbs I have ever seen!" Pierre proclaimed. "Not to mention an *exceptionnel* epithelium, *merveilleux* mitral cells, and a *grande* glomerulus!"

"What's he talking about?" Mumps asked.

"He's admiring the different components of Schnoz's world-class olfactory system," Vivian answered.

"The man sure is an expert on noses," Jimmy said. "He and Schnoz should get along great."

While Pierre gazed lovingly at my nasal anatomy, my thoughts drifted toward Jean Paul Puanteur. He was my all-time favorite perfumer and the reason I was here. His picture was on the cover of the exhibition's program, and he was to be the closing night keynote speaker at PerfumeCon. My snot bubbled with excitement at the thought of finally meeting him.

"Le Nez, you are just what I am looking for," Pierre announced, flicking off the penlight.

"What's 'le Nez' mean?" TJ asked.

"Nose," Arnaud chimed in.

"I don't understand," I said, a bit confused. "Why are you looking for my nose?"

"To assist me, *jeune homme*," Pierre said.

"What did he say?" TJ asked again.

"*Jeune homme* means 'young man' in French," Dr. Wackjöb clarified.

"Assist you in doing what?" I questioned.

Pierre let out a loud belly laugh. "Smelling, *odeur*!"

From the sound of it, *odeur* sounded a lot like 'odor' in English. That meant he wanted me to use my nose, or *nez*, to smell something. I was beginning to pick up on a few words in the French language.

"I would like you to come to my perfume laboratory on West Thirtieth Street so I can witness your *phénoménal* nose in action," Pierre continued. "I have several new lines of perfumes, and I would love to get your opinion on which ones smell the best."

My heart skipped a beat, and my nose hairs pricked with anticipation. A professional perfumer actually wanted me to smell his new line of perfumes!

"Vivian!" I gushed. "Quickly, tweak my nostrils to see if I'm dreaming!"

"You're wide awake," Vivian said. "The man really wants you to smell some of his creations."

I looked to Dr. Wackjöb for permission. He was, after all, our adult chaperone for the trip.

"It is fine by me," he said. "Shall we all go?"

"No way," Jimmy protested. "I don't want to go to some perfume laboratory and watch Schnoz smell stuff."

"Me either," Mumps chimed in.

"We see Schnoz sniff things all time," TJ added.

"This is an invitation for le Nez only," Pierre said. "I mean, you are in New York, the most exciting city in the world—after Paris. Enjoy the sights. Besides, I wouldn't want to bore you with lines of perfume still in their *enfance* stage."

"How will we all meet up for dinner?" Dr. Wackjöb wondered.

"Dinner is on me, Aðalbjörn," Pierre offered. "I will send Arnaud to your hotel at seven o'clock. You will all join me for dinner at Nourriture, the finest French restaurant in New York."

"Does that mean we'll be eating french fries?" Mumps asked.

"We will have a *délicieux* three-course meal, beginning with *salade verte* and *la soupe à l'oignon*," Arnaud rattled off. "Next, you will have a choice between *les coquilles Saint-Jacques à la Provençal, le saumon d'ecosse,* or *les filets de bœuf.* Dessert will be *la tarte fine aux pommes* or *crème brulée à la vanille.* I have arranged everything."

TJ leaned over and whispered in my ear. "What's he talking about? That sounds like the most disgusting food ever."

"I hope those words mean hamburgers, hot dogs, and pepperoni pizza in French," Mumps said.

"I doubt it," Vivian said. "But I think *bœuf* means 'beef.' Sorry, there's no way I'm eating a dead animal. I'm a strict vegetarian."

Just then, a bunch of people carrying notebooks and iPads burst into the gallery. They were dressed in normal-looking street clothes, not fancy tuxedoes and evening gowns like those that everybody else was wearing.

"Who are they?" Vivian wondered.

"*Journalistes,*" Pierre announced. "They have come to interview the great Pierre du Voleur!"

Arnaud straightened Pierre's bow tie and plucked lint from his tuxedo jacket. The *journalistes* hurried in our direction, pen and notebooks poised for writing, iPads charged and ready to go.

Just as the first reporter was about to ask Pierre a question, a flurry of activity broke out behind us. I turned around and saw a short man with thick, curly gray hair step into the gallery. He also wore a black tuxedo, but instead of fancy black shoes, he had on a pair of bright red Converse sneakers.

Jean Paul Puanteur!

The man, the myth, the perfuming legend was standing less than ten feet from me! I instantly recognized his face from the picture of him in my room. When the *journalistes* saw Jean Paul, they completely ignored Pierre and flocked to the creator of Strange.

Voices rang out.

"Jean Paul, look this way for photo!"

"I love Strange!"

"Tell us your secret of Strange success!"

"Mr. Puanteur, give us a quote!"

"I have only one thing to say before I let my fragrance do the talking," Jean Paul said in a deep voice heavy with French inflection. "Strange is as Strange does."

A series of astonished *oohs* and *ahhs* escaped

from the *journalistes'* lips, like Jean Paul had just given them the secret of the universe or something. The ones holding pens quickly scribbled down the quote. Others checked their iPads, making double sure they had digitally captured his words.

I took three deep snorts, trying to work up the courage to introduce myself, when Pierre's normally pale complexion suddenly flamed fiery red. "Jean Paul Puanteur is a fake, a fraud, and an *escroc* of the highest order!" he screamed.

Jean Paul looked up from the reporters and glared at Pierre. "Pierre du Voleur! Get that *crasseux* rat out of my sight! He belongs in the gutter, not a museum!"

Pierre lunged at Jean Paul, his fists curled and ready to fight. But before he could throw a punch, a burly bodyguard wearing dark sunglasses pushed him aside and escorted Jean Paul out of the exhibition hall.

"What was that all about?" I cried.

"You will know soon enough," Pierre huffed as he and Arnaud tugged me toward an awaiting car.

CHAPTER 10

THE FRANÇAIS SCENT COMPANY

Before I snapped on my seat belt, Arnaud shifted the car into drive and sped recklessly through the city streets. Pierre's reaction to Jean Paul inside the museum had taken me by surprise. I was curious to know why he wanted to fight my hero, but I dared not ask him. The man had yet to calm down. His face was still as red as a cherry popsicle, and I could see a vein on his temple throbbing a million miles an hour.

After a wild ten-minute ride and two near-collisions, Arnaud skidded to a stop in front of a dingy-looking brick building.

"We are here," Pierre said. "Follow me."

An attendant opened the doors, and we walked inside. I knew from reading magazine articles that the perfume business was all about style, fashion, and making a great first impression. So, I was expecting Pierre to overwhelm me with an opulent lobby—perhaps a white marble floor, slick modern furniture, and a bunch of young assistants answering phones. Instead, the first floor looked more like the waiting room of my ENT (ear, nose, and throat) doctor's office. The carpet was an ugly, algae-green color. Four mismatched folding chairs sat against the wood-panel wall. Hanging precariously above the lobby attendant's desk was a fading sign that read: *Français Scent Company—American Headquarters.*

Pierre and Arnaud ushered me into a creaky elevator. When the doors opened to the third floor, an unpleasant blast of artificial, synthetic scents bombarded my olfactory bulbs. The smells were nothing like the organic, natural scents locked inside Strange.

"Arnaud, show le Nez around for a moment,"

Pierre said. "I need to make a quick phone call." He then disappeared into a small office, slamming the door behind him.

"Pierre doesn't seem too happy," I remarked.

"Monsieur du Voleur has good reason not to be happy," Arnaud said.

"Why?"

"All of his best work has been systematically stolen by one man."

"Who?"

"Jean Paul Puanteur."

I couldn't believe my ears. Jean Paul Puanteur, the world's greatest scent artist, a thief? "Why in the world would he steal perfume ideas from Pierre?" I wondered aloud.

"The so-called darling of the perfuming world is an untalented *escroc*. That is why.

"What's 'ace...crock' mean? I've heard that word used to describe Jean Paul twice today."

"*Escroc* means 'crook, thief, trickster' in English. Let's not talk about Puanteur anymore. Just the mention of his name sends Monsieur du Voleur's blood pressure to *dangereux* levels."

I kept my mouth shut while Arnaud gave me a tour of the Français Scent Company's perfume laboratory. Unfortunately, I couldn't keep my nose shut, because the place stunk to high heaven with dozens of yucky synthetic aroma compounds. I had sniffed the nastiest odors in the world—the Gates of Smell, hákarl, roadkill skunk on the side of the road—but a whiff of any artificial scent made my nose hairs recoil.

Still, I collected the fake musk for inclusion in my mental scent dictionary. My nostrils scooped up semi-toxic substances like musk ketone, musk xylene, galaxolide, and tonalide. I knew from reading that those chemicals were potentially dangerous to humans, especially galaxolide and tonalide.

"This is where the magic of the Français Scent Company happens," Arnaud said, leading me through a set of double doors and into a large room.

The room was white and sterile-looking, a complete contrast to the dreariness of the rest of the building. One side of the room had long tables piled with hundreds of small brown bottles. Two bored-looking men and one equally disinterested woman wearing lab coats sat on swivel stools, dipping little wooden sticks into the bottles and then smelling them.

A vast array of chemical-laced aromas wafted in the air. My sniffer picked up scents like baked pumpkin, pomegranate jam, ripe papaya, banana peel, apricot, campfire marshmallow, and dozens of other imitation aromas.

"Are those people perfumers?" I asked Arnaud.

"They are my fragrance technicians," a voice bellowed from behind me. "But compared to you, le Nez, their noses are about as useless as a skunk without stink spray."

I turned and saw Pierre. His face was no longer red, and the throbbing vein on his temple had calmed to a normal pulse. Oddly enough, he was clutching a fancy gift bag with Jean Paul Puanteur's Strange logo emblazoned in gilded script.

"I created *Bête Blanc*—White Beast, my most popular perfume, in this very room," Pierre continued. "It was the second most preferred fragrance of incarcerated females in the United States prison system from 2001 to 2003."

"The number one most popular prisoner perfume of the time was Évasion by You-know-who," Arnaud said.

Pierre shot him a dirty look.

"What's that huge machine in the corner?" I asked.

"A robotic mixer," Pierre explained. "We use it to blend ingredients to create new *parfums*. I want your exquisite *nez* to sniff several new lines we are currently working on."

"How do you capture the smells of natural, living flowers to use in your perfumes?"

Pierre chuckled and then shot Arnaud a sly look. "Le Nez, this is the twenty-first century," he said. "We buy our scents from Khasabu Fragrance and Flavor International in India. They are the world's largest—and cheapest—synthetic scent manufacturers in the world."

"Only fools like Jean Paul Puanteur use all-natural ingredients," Arnaud added. "They cost a fortune and cut deeply into his profits."

The word *escroc* flashed in my mind—crook, thief, trickster. I needed to know the truth about Jean Paul, but I could tell from the look on Pierre's face that this was not the time to bring up the subject.

"What do you want me to smell first?" I asked.

"I thought you'd never ask," Pierre said. He then placed the gift bag he was holding on a table and pulled from it a very familiar-looking red bottle.

"Strange," he said with a wicked smile. "I want you to smell Strange."

CHAPTER 11

NEZ PROFESSIONNEL

"Why would you want me to smell Strange?" I asked, a bit confused by Pierre's request. "Don't you want me to sniff some of *your* perfumes?"

Pierre looked at his watch and then clapped his hands, getting the attention of the three fragrance technicians who were working at a back table. "*Madame et messieurs*, you can leave two hours early today. You will be compensated for a full day's work."

"Thank you, *merci*," the excited fragrance technicians echoed as they grabbed their jackets and hurried out of the lab.

"Arnaud, I need to speak with you in my office for a moment," Pierre said. "Le Nez, we will be right back."

A sudden quiet fell over the Français Scent Company. The events of the day replayed in my mind—the gondola trip from New Hampshire to New York City, landing on top of a skyscraper, the Art of Odor exhibit, and seeing Jean Paul Puanteur up close and personal. Now, less than eight hours after I had lifted off from Jimmy's backyard, I was alone inside a professional perfumer's laboratory. I still found the odor of synthetic fragrances a bit disgusting, but I was finally in a place where a kid with a big nose and a sense of smell like a dog was an honored guest instead of an object of ridicule.

The laboratory door swung open. Pierre strolled into the room followed by Arnaud, who was carrying a large sheet of paper in one hand and a fancy quill pen in the other.

"Le Nez," Pierre announced. "I want to make you the richest nose in the world."

"Huh?" I mumbled, flaring my nostrils.

"Show him, Arnaud."

Arnaud placed an official-looking scroll of paper in front of me.

"What is it?" I asked.

"An employment contract," Pierre answered. "I want you to work for me."

"I already have a job. Every Sunday the Denmark Parks and Rec Department pays me a dollar for every pile of dog poop I sniff out that people have neglected to pick up. Dog waste left on the ground near the town's swimming pond causes pollution problems."

Pierre laughed. "I am talking about a real job. In fact, one of the most important jobs in the whole perfume industry— a *nez professionnel!*

I scratched my sniffer and thought for a second. *Nez* meant 'nose.' *Professionnel* sounded a lot like 'professional.' "Are you saying that you want to hire me as a professional nose?"

"*Oui,*" Pierre said. "You will be a very highly compensated *nez professionnel.* Read the number at the bottom of the contract."

I looked down at the paper, skimming through the boring parts until finally focusing on a number with a bunch of zeroes at the end.

"One million dollars!" I exclaimed. "Is this a typo or something?"

"It is no mistake," Pierre said. "One million dollars will be yours."

All the things I could buy with that kind of money tumbled around in my brain. Personal rock-climbing gym in my backyard. A brand-new, state-of-the-art underground hideout for Vivian, the Not-Right Brothers, and me. Custom-made Mardi Gras masks decorated with gold leaf. Pencil sharpeners shaped like big noses to hand out as gag gifts at school. Nuclear-powered nose hair clippers and an endless supply of high-grade cayenne pepper imported from Peru. The possibilities were endless!

But most of all, I could help my parents repair all of the damage to our house that my earthquake-like snoring had caused.

"Give me a pen!" I whooped. "I'll sign right here and now!"

"In due time," Pierre said. "First, you will need to pass a smell test."

"What kind of smell test?"

Arnaud placed a bunch of bottles of perfume on the table. I recognized most of them from the Art of Odor exhibit. Famous scents like Dracula Noir, Sticky, Appetite, Perhaps, and Mammal No. 5.

"I want you to sniff each perfume and then tell me the precise ingredients," Pierre instructed. "A *nez professionnel* knows every smell in the world and is prized for his or her skilled and intelligent assessment of fragrances."

"In other words," Arnaud added, "you need to name every scent in the bottles or you get nothing."

Pierre looked at his watch. "This test will be timed. Do you have any questions?"

I shook my head, no.

"Then you may begin now!"

A jolt of anxiety shot through my body. My fingers shook as I popped the cap from the first perfume—Sticky by Jacques Gluant. The scent wafted from the bottle and into my awaiting honker.

"I smell bergamot, lavender, amber, civet," I rattled off. "And a slight hint of lemon."

"Perfect!" Pierre gushed. "Quickly, smell another one."

I grabbed the bottle of Dracula Noir by Otto Sang, twisted off the cap, and took a huge whiff. "Off the top, I smell rosemary, basil, lemon, bergamot, and cinnamon. Then subtle hints of leather, amber, pine, and sandalwood."

"Excellent!" Pierre exclaimed. "You are an aromatic genius, an *odeur* prodigy! Now, smell the bottle of Mammal No. 5."

For the next fifteen minutes, I astonished Pierre and Arnaud with my olfactory gifts. I systematically listed every fragrance in every bottle of perfume they placed in front of me. The hard work I had put into my mental scent dictionary paid off, and now it was going to reward me with a million dollars. I couldn't wait to see my parents' faces when I handed them a wad of cash to patch the foundation of our house!

"When do I get paid?" I asked, still dreaming of ways to spend the money.

"Not so fast, le Nez," Pierre muttered. "We still have one more perfume."

He placed the bottle of Strange on the table. My heart skipped a beat, and a bead of sweat dripped from my forehead all the way down the bridge of my nose. With the excitement of being in a real perfume lab and getting a million dollars, I had forgotten all about my inability to huff out the secret scent of Strange.

"Scent dictionary, don't fail me," I prayed and then took a big snort of Strange. "There are essential oils like lavender, jasmine, more sandalwood, and bergamot," I said with a shaky voice. "And I get mild hints of artemisia, coriander, patchouli, carnation, and one final scent is...uh...um."

"What is it?" Pierre growled in my face. "I need to know the final ingredient or you say *au revoir* to the *millions de dollars!*"

My nervous nostrils quivered like a cell phone switched on vibrate. Frantically, I scanned my mental scent dictionary, silently pleading for the odor to reveal itself. The vanilla-like smell was earthy yet sophisticated, the icing on the most deliciously perfect perfume ever concocted by man.

"Tell me the scent!" Pierre demanded.

"It's...it's...I don't know!" I cried out, tears

streaming down my face. "It resembles vanilla but none I've ever smelled before!"

Pierre grabbed more bottles and bags of dried bean pods from a shelf. "These are all of the synthetic and natural vanilla essences known to man," he said. "Do you smell one of these?"

Inhaling deeply, I sniffed vanilla beans from Mexico, Tahiti, and Madagascar. There was no match. I moved quickly to the bottles—vanilla extract, pure vanilla extract, and vanilla essence. Again, there was no match. Lastly, I popped the cap on a bottle of vanillin, the synthetic version of vanilla. The unnatural ingredients made my nose turn away in disgust.

"It's none of these," I informed him. "The unknown, vanilla-like ingredient in Strange is from a completely different origin."

Pierre violently slammed his fist on the table, sending bottles crashing to the floor. "You are a failure!" he screamed, his face flaming red and his temple vein throbbing. "You will never be a *nez professionnel,* and you will never see a penny of the money until you figure out every single ingredient inside Strange. Come with me, Arnaud. I need to get ready for our *dîner* with Aðalbjörn and his friends."

Pierre and Arnaud walked out of the lab, leaving me alone. I laid my nose on the table, feeling horrible because I had let Pierre down. I was a complete sniffing loser, and it was all because of Strange.

CHAPTER 12

UNTALENTED INSECTE

Pierre, Arnaud, and I drove to the restaurant in silence. The two of them were so disappointed in my inability to conquer Strange that they wouldn't even look at me. My dream job as a *nez professionnel* and the million dollars were slipping away.

"We have arrived," Arnaud said, wheeling to the curb.

I looked out of the car's tinted windows. Dr. Wackjöb, Vivian, and the Not-Right Brothers were waiting on the sidewalk under a big sign that read: *Nourriture—Cuisine Française.*

"Do not mention anything about what happened

in the perfume lab this afternoon," Pierre ordered before we stepped out of the car. "I have not given up on you yet, le Nez. I have faith that you will tell me the secret of Strange, and the *millions de dollars* will be yours."

Pierre patted my shoulder and smiled at me. My nostrils swelled with relief. He wasn't mad at me anymore! There was still a chance for me to sniff out Strange and show him the power of my proboscis. I hopped out of the car and walked into the restaurant with my friends.

While Pierre and Dr. Wackjöb chatted, Vivian and the Not-Right Brothers told me about their afternoon touring New York City.

"After the Art of Odor, we went to the top of the Empire State Building," Jimmy said, biting into a breadstick. "The view was awesome!"

Mumps pointed to greasy splotch on his skull. "This is where a pigeon pooped on my head."

"Yuck." I grimaced. "You could have at least washed it off."

"Not a chance. It's supposed to be good luck. Plus, I'm keeping it there as a souvenir to show my little brother."

"Tomorrow we're going to the Museum of Natural History," TJ said. "There's a living spider exhibit that I have to see. Black widows, tarantulas, wolf spiders, hairy scorpions, giant vinegaroons, the brown recluse, and the deadliest creepy-crawly in the world—the Brazilian wandering spider!"

Jimmy shuddered. "Spiders give me the creeps."

"Maybe one will bite you," Vivian joked. "Then you'll become Spider Boy!"

We all laughed.

"How was your afternoon of sniffing perfumes?" Dr. Wackjöb asked me.

Pierre stared at me, his intense gaze like sharp needles plunging up my nose holes.

I lowered my head, unable to look Dr. Wackjöb in the eye. "It was fun," I muttered. "Pierre has some awesome new fragrances coming out."

After parking the car, Arnaud joined us at the table. Since he had preordered our meal, we didn't get to pick from a menu. Our first course—*salade verte* and *la soupe à l'oignon*—was really a hunk of iceberg lettuce with some tomatoes and a cup of onion soup. I could do without the salad, but the soup was okay. I love the smell of onions.

Next was the main course. Our choices were *les coquilles Saint-Jacques à la Provencal, le saumon d'ecosse,* or *les filets de bœuf.* We quickly learned that *coquilles Saint-Jacques* were scallops, *saumon d'ecosse* meant Scottish salmon, and *filets de bœuf* was beef. The Not-Right Brothers and I picked beef. Dr. Wackjöb and Pierre ordered the salmon, and Arnaud had the scallops. Vivian just got a refill of salad, bread sticks, and onion soup.

"Le Nez," Pierre addressed me through a mouthful of baked salmon. "I would like you to return to my perfume laboratory again tomorrow morning. Your astute observations of my fragrances were quite impressive. Is this okay with you, Aðalbjörn?"

Dr. Wackjöb shrugged. "It's fine with me. I can tell how much Schnoz enjoyed spending time with you."

"But you'll miss all the deadly spiders at the Museum of Natural History," TJ said.

"Plus, I wanted Schnoz to help me coax another

pigeon into pooping on my head so I could have double good luck," Mumps complained.

"We're going to miss you," Vivian added.

This was a golden chance to get out of another tortuous session of Strange smelling. The stress of trying to figure out the mystery scent was too much, and I needed a break. "You guys are right," I said. "I should spend the day with you, visiting all the—"

"Nonsense," Dr. Wackjöb said. "The Museum of Natural History is not going anywhere, and we still have four full days in New York. Schnoz, spending one more day with a professional perfumer like Pierre is the chance of a lifetime."

My nostrils deflated and I felt a little icky, like a pigeon had just pooped all over *my* head. Before I could protest, a hard glance from Arnaud caught my attention. He raised his right hand, rubbed his thumb and fingertips together, and made the international sign for money.

One million dollars.

The dough was just a single smell away. If I could sniff out the secret of Strange, I could take care of my family forever. I cleared my throat to get everyone's attention and raised my water glass in the air.

"A toast to Pierre and the fabulous fragrances of the Français Scent Company," I declared. "For making my perfuming dreams come true."

The sound of tinkling glasses filled the air. Pierre was enjoying his dessert of *la tarte fine aux pommes*—apple tart—when the restaurant doors opened and in walked a familiar-looking man wearing a black tuxedo with bright red Converse sneakers.

Jean Paul Puanteur!

A man wearing a name tag that read *Maître D'* welcomed Jean Paul to the restaurant by kissing him on both cheeks. A small entourage, including his two burly bodyguards, joined him at a choice table next to a fancy stained-glass window.

Pierre dropped his spoon, wiped his mouth, and groaned, "I have suddenly lost my *appétit*. Please excuse me, Aðalbjörn. I have urgent business to attend. Le Nez, I will send Arnaud to pick you up at your hotel at nine a.m. sharp." He paid for the meal, and then he and Arnaud disappeared into the city streets.

"This was just like at the Art of Odor," Vivian commented. "As soon as Jean Paul Puanteur enters, Pierre du Voleur decides it's time to leave."

"I hope we're not leaving," TJ said. "I haven't even finished my apple tart."

"I remember Pierre always being a bit odd during our college days," Dr. Wackjöb said, taking a sip of coffee. "But eat your desserts, children. We will stay until you have finished your meal."

Seeing Jean Paul made my nose hairs knot. I still found it hard to believe that he had stolen Pierre's perfumes. This was my chance to meet the man. Maybe I'd have the opportunity to ask him about secret scent so I could be a millionaire! I excused myself from the table and headed in the direction of the bathroom. When I got near his table, I took three quick huffs to calm my nerves and stepped next to his chair.

Instantly, his two bodyguards bolted to attention, ready to escort me away from their boss. Jean Paul, however, waved them off and stared intently at the mass of fleshy cartilage in the middle of my face.

"My name is…uh…Andy…Schnoz…le Nez," I stuttered. "I am a huge fan of Strange and wanted to…uh…say…um…"

Jean Paul stood up before I finished my bumbling sentence. He was shorter than I had thought. The top of his curly gray hair barely reached the tip

of my schnozola. And then, like a man examining a piece of rare, exquisite pottery, he reached out with both hands and gently stroked my honker.

"Beautiful," he said softly. "You have a *nez* that puts other *nez* to shame."

"My nose can smell great too," I said. "I know your signature perfume, Strange, has an awesome blend of lavender, jasmine, sandalwood, bergamot, patchouli, and stuff like that. But there's another very subtle, mysterious scent in the mixture that my *nez* can't quite figure out. What is it?"

The master perfumer frowned and shook his head disapprovingly. "When I arrived at the restaurant, I noticed you were sitting with that untalented *insecte*, Pierre du Voleur. Tell him that he has stooped to a new low by using an *écolier*, a schoolboy, to try and steal my creations. Now, leave me alone. I am having *dîner*."

Jean Paul's bodyguards ordered me to step away from the table. As I walked back to the gang, my head and snout felt woozy. Jean Paul and Pierre were accusing each other of swiping fragrances, and I didn't know which man to believe.

CHAPTER 13

WHO WANTS TO SMELL A MILLIONAIRE?

I tossed and turned in bed all night long, and it wasn't because of Mumps farting in his sleep. My mind raced with images of Jean Paul, Pierre, and Strange. The two perfumers were obviously rivals, and I was stuck in the middle of their fragrance feud right up to my world-class nostrils.

As the first slivers of sun peeked over the New York City skyline, I heard a knock at my hotel room door. I instantly whipped off the blanket and looked at the clock—5:44 a.m. Arnaud, I thought right away. He must have come early to pick me up for another day of Strange sniffing at the Français Scent Company.

"Schnoz, are you up?" a voice whispered from the hallway.

It was Vivian.

I pulled on a pair of jeans, slipped on a T-shirt, and opened the door. "What are you doing up so early?" I asked her.

"I couldn't sleep."

"Me neither."

"There are a couple of chairs in the foyer next to the vending machines down the hall. Let's go. We need to talk."

Vivian slipped a couple dollars into the vending machine and punched up two packs of peanut butter crackers. "Breakfast is on me," she said, handing me the crackers. "Now, let's not beat around the boogers. What is wrong with you?"

"Nothing's wrong with me," I said. "Whatever gave you that idea?"

"Something's on your mind. Last night at dinner, you looked like a stressed-out lab monkey during a psychological experiment."

I let out a deep snort and stared at the ceiling. "I like your analogy, because that's exactly what I feel like."

"Then tell me what's bothering you."

"Okay. But you have to promise not to say anything."

"You can trust me," she said, and then pretended to lock her lips with an imaginary key.

"I'm one sniff away from being a millionaire," I blurted out.

Vivian cocked her head and raised her eyebrows. "A sniff away from a million *what?*"

"One million dollars! Currency, bread, cash, and whatever the French word for money is."

"*Argent* is the French word for cash. I learned that at the restaurant last night."

"Whatever. Pierre said he would pay me a million dollars if I could list every ingredient in a bunch of perfumes. That's what I was doing at his perfume lab yesterday. I guessed every one until I had to smell Strange. When I couldn't figure out the secret ingredient, Pierre got so mad I thought he was going to hit me."

Vivian sat up and paced the hallway, index finger tapping her chin, trying to make sense of what I had just told her. "Did Pierre tell you *why* he had to know every ingredient in Strange?"

"To see if I was ready for a job," I said, biting into a peanut butter cracker. "He wants to hire me."

"Hire you for what? You already have a job sniffing out dog poop in the park."

"He wants me to be his *nez professionnel*. That means "professional nose" in English. It's one of the most important and highly compensated jobs in the perfume industry. The test was to see if I had the smelling chops to perform all the duties."

"Since you couldn't figure out the secret of Strange, you failed the test, right?"

"Yes, but he's giving me another chance today."

Vivian paced around some more, still tapping her chin and practically wearing a hole in the carpet. While she marched, I filled her in on every detail—from the offer of a million dollars and smelling all the perfumes to Pierre's anger issues. I wasn't ready to tell her Jean Paul and Pierre had accused each other of stealing fragrances.

"Schnoz, this is the sniffing opportunity of a lifetime!" Vivian exclaimed. "Think about it. You can get a million big ones just for figuring out a simple smell. It's like you're a contestant on that TV game show *Who Wants to Be a Millionaire?*"

"More like *Who Wants to* Smell *a Millionaire?*" I countered.

Vivian laughed. "I say go for it. You have nothing to lose and everything to gain."

"But what if I can't figure out the smell? Then I get nothing."

"Schnoz, think about it. Yesterday at this time, you were standing in Jimmy's backyard in New Hampshire struggling to lift a gondola off the ground. A day later, you're in New York City and a perfuming company has offered you a job and a million dollars if you can figure out a dumb odor. You're the Cinderella of smells!"

Vivian was right. Strange was my glass slipper and the million dollars my happily ever after. But I knew that every fairy tale had a villain. Who was my Evil Stepmother—Pierre, Arnaud, Jean Paul, or Strange itself?

"Thanks for cheering me up," I told her. "This is the experience of a lifetime. And if I can't figure out the smell and don't get the million dollars, no big deal. I never had it to lose in the first place."

"Now you're thinking like a superhero," Vivian said, cupping a hand to her mouth to cover a yawn. "I'm going back to bed."

We parted ways and went back to our rooms. When I opened the door, Mumps was still asleep and tooting away under the blankets like a bad trombone player. I plopped down on my bed and reviewed my mental scent dictionary. Each delicious scent was alphabetized, categorized, and organized like a virtual public library. The secret of Strange was hiding somewhere inside my honker, and today was the day I would reveal its fragrance.

THE BOATHOUSE

A couple hours later, I met the gang in the hotel restaurant for breakfast.

"After we eat, we're heading straight for the Museum of Natural History," TJ mumbled through a mouthful of oatmeal.

"Then we're going to the Central Park Zoo," Mumps added.

Dr. Wackjöb held up his empty cup, signaling to the server that he'd like more coffee. "We wish you could be with us," the doctor said, splashing milk into his refill. "But I know how much your time with Pierre is worth to you."

"It's worth a million bucks!" Vivian blurted out.

"What do you mean a *million bucks?*" Jimmy asked.

My nostrils flared with anger. I shot Vivian a dirty look. The girl had promised to keep the million dollars a secret, and two hours hadn't passed before she let the snot out of the sack.

"It's just a figure of speech," Vivian said quickly after realizing what she had done. "You know, it's an experience that money can't buy."

"I'd buy a lot of experiences with a million dollars," TJ mused.

"Like what?" Mumps asked.

"First, I'd buy us a big jet and fly us around the world!"

Jimmy pointed to my nose. "We already have a jet, and it's plastered right in the middle of Schnoz's face. He sailed us all the way from New Hampshire to New York with just a few sniffs of cayenne pepper fueling his solid rocket boogers. If we loaded his honker with enough cayenne, he could probably fly us to the moon and back!"

The restaurant door opened, and Arnaud stepped inside.

"My ride is here," I said.

"Have a great day of smelling Strange," Vivian said with a wink.

I chugged down the rest of my orange juice, said good-bye to my friends, and hopped in the backseat of Arnaud's car. I was surprised when we sped past the Français Scent Company's bland brick building.

"Where are we going?" I asked.

"Monsieur du Voleur thought a change of scenery might be better for your *nez*," Arnaud explained. "He has rented a private space for the day inside the Boathouse in Central Park."

"What's the Boathouse?"

"It is an *exquis* restaurant and oasis in the middle of the city. You can rent boats and bicycles by the hour. You can also rent private dining rooms. Monsieur du Voleur has reserved one for you."

I shrugged, not caring where the final smell test would take place. The only thing that concerned me was figuring out the mystery ingredient in Strange and getting my million. Arnaud wheeled

the car into a parking garage. We then entered
Central Park at Seventy-Second Street and Fifth
Avenue on foot and strolled down a path toward
the Boathouse.

Five minutes later, we came upon a lake. I remembered the body of water instantly. It was the
same place where I had almost landed the gondola
when we first arrived in New York. Rowboats for
rent bobbed in the water along a wooden dock.
Arnaud led me into a large building with a fancy
green roof and a large outdoor terrace for dining.

"Do you have a reservation?" a hostess wearing
a white shirt and flowing black skirt asked us.

"We have one in the name of Pierre du Voleur,"
Arnaud said. "It is for a private room, party of three."

"Yes, of course," the hostess said. "Mr. du Voleur
is waiting for you. Please, follow me."

The hostess led us through a packed dining
area and into a small room with an awesome view
of the lake and even better view of the skyscrapers
towering over the trees in the distance.

"Le Nez," Pierre said, shaking my hand as I
entered the room. "I am so glad you could join us.

Voulez-vous le petit déjeuner?" He motioned toward a buffet table loaded with fruit, cheese, croissants, and a large jar of Nutella.

I raised my eyebrows, not sure what Pierre had just asked me.

"He wants to know if you would like breakfast," Arnaud clarified.

"No, I'm good. I just ate at the hotel."

"Very well," Pierre said. "Now, let's get down to business."

A small round table with a single chair sat next to a window that overlooked the lake. Sitting in the center on a white tablecloth was a brand-new bottle of Strange.

"The moment has arrived, le Nez," Pierre said to me. "Today, you become a *nez professionnel*, an *odeur artiste* with such an acute sense of smell that you can compose complex fragrances that convey intense moods, deep feelings, and wonderful sensations."

"Don't forget about my million dollars," I reminded him.

Pierre smiled. "I will be back in fifteen minutes.

You will then reveal to me the secret of Strange, or you don't get a penny."

The two men then walked outside and closed the door behind them. I sat down at the table, just my nose and a rosy bottle of Strange. Like two MMA fighters ready to duke it out for the ultimate prize. My heart raced, nostrils quivered, fingers shook as I twisted off the cap. Instantly, familiar smells wafted in the air: lavender, jasmine, sandalwood, bergamot.

One last scent escaped from the bottle—the mystery ingredient, the phantom fragrance, the million-dollar odor dancing around my nose like an aromatic apparition. I huffed and snorted with all my olfactory might. The vanilla-like smell penetrated my scent receptors, flooding my mental scent dictionary. I frantically searched for the musk's origin like a computer program scanning for a rogue virus.

"Earthy…grass…dirt…" I gasped. "Something definitely found on the ground, yet totally sweet and intoxicating. The secret of Strange is…I don't know!"

I slammed my nose violently on the table.

The glass bottle of Strange flew on the floor and splintered into a thousand shards. The mysterious scent was everywhere, mocking me, teasing my nose worse than any playground bully ever had. Tears formed in my eyes. I looked out the window and saw Pierre and Arnaud walking toward the Boathouse.

Before I had to face the men with my failure, I tore out of the room and raced into the heart of Central Park.

CHAPTER 15

THE SECRET
OF STRANGE

The Central Park Zoo.

Mumps had mentioned at breakfast that the gang would head to the zoo after visiting the Museum of Natural History. I stopped and asked directions from an old guy who was feeding stale bread to pigeons.

"Zoo's that way," he grumbled, pointing in a southeast direction. "Sixty-Fourth and Fifth."

"Thanks," I said, and then tore off down a path.

While I ran, I looked over my shoulder every few yards to see if Pierre and Arnaud were following me. They were nowhere in sight. When I arrived at the zoo, I checked the time on a clock mounted to a brick wall—ten thirty-five.

It was way too early for Vivian, the Not-Right Brothers, and Dr. Wackjöb to be at the zoo. They were still touring the Museum of Natural History and probably wouldn't even show up until after lunch. My only choice was to wait for them, so I purchased a ticket and pushed through the turnstile.

Like throughout the rest of New York, the smell of Strange completely permeated the zoo. I even saw the gift shop manager spraying himself with the stuff when I was browsing through a book of endangered animals. Using the zoo map, I scooted down a walkway and entered the Tropic Zone.

The exhibit featured creatures found in the Earth's rain forests. Black and white lemurs leaped through a canopy above my head. Colorful birds with names like golden weaver, Victoria crowned pigeon, and white-rumped shama flitted from branch to branch. A creepy-looking orange-and-yellow snake called a macabrel sat curled in a corner.

The next animal I saw stopped me in my

tracks. A creature called a big-nosed tamandua— otherwise known as an anteater. My animal spirit had sandy fur with striking black markings. The shape of our noses was surprisingly similar. Long, pointy, and fat with a set of huge, flaring nostrils. The anteater flicked its lengthy pink tongue and then stared at me. Its black eyes were intense and glistening, like it was trying to communicate with me.

BIG-NOSED
TAMANDUA
ANTEATER

"Can you smell Strange, little guy?" I whispered. "I bet if you talked, you'd tell me the secret."

The ear-piercing screech of a wild-haired golden lion tamarin shattered our bond. The anteater flicked its tongue one last time and then scurried out of sight behind a big rock. I moved out of the Tropic Zone and headed for the Sea Lion Pool. A trio of seals swam, splashed, and sunned themselves on rocks. A bunch of little kids made barking sounds, trying to get the seals to answer back.

Temperate Territory, the next exhibit, was filled with snow monkeys, snow leopards, red pandas, turtles, and big, white wading birds. The highlight here was the salty, ammonia tang of snow leopard pee. The unique urine odor of this elusive cat native to the Himalayan Mountains was fresh and new. I quickly added it to my mental scent dictionary.

I breezed through the Polar Zone (the penguins and puffins were kind of boring) and entered the final exhibit called Camels—Ships of the Desert. The first type I saw was an Arabian camel, also known as a dromedary because it only has one hump. A sign posted on the fence warned that camels were notorious for spitting at zoo patrons, so be aware. I had never smelled camel spit before and was actually hoping one would expectorate in my direction. Today wasn't my lucky day, however, because the animals were all too busy munching on dried hay and small brown pellets to notice me.

A tired-looking mother pushing a baby carriage with one hand and clutching a toddler with the other strolled up beside me.

"Mommy, want ride camel," the toddler garbled.

A zoo attendant, who was inside the enclosure scattering food for the camels to eat, wandered over to us. "Camel rides are on the main lawn from noon to three p.m.," she explained. "Cost is ten dollars a ride including photos. You can purchase tickets inside the gift shop."

The mother said thanks and walked away. The attendant went back to her work of feeding and watering the animals.

I moved farther down the fence and came to another type of camel called a Bactrian, native to the Gobi Desert in Mongolia. There was only one, and it was a lot hairier than the Arabian type and had two humps instead of one. I was about to head toward the Dancing Crane Café for a bite to eat when I noticed a smell—or a lack of smell, to be more precise.

The overpowering potpourri of Strange was fading away, but the single, earthy, vanilla-like ingredient inside the perfume was fuming hard and heavy inside my nostrils. I squeezed my schnozola between the fence's metal gates and sniffed deeply. There was no mistaking it—the secret ingredient of Strange was drifting inside the Bactrian camel enclosure!

I had to get inside and investigate. But how could I do it? The fence was at least ten feet high. Plus, the zoo attendant was still wandering around. The sudden urge to eat some candy came over me. I was reaching into my pocket for a piece when a sudden gust of wind swept through my hair. My nostrils inflated and my toes lifted off the ground.

"I'm flying," I said with a grin, and then floated gently over the fence and landed quietly next to a watering trough.

The attendant was a few feet away with her back to me, completely unaware of my presence. However, the huge Bactrian camel noticed me right away. It hoofed over, gave me a quick sniff, and then let loose a wad of frothing camel spit right in my face.

"Ugh!" I yelped, wiping camel saliva out of my eyes. "Be careful what you wish for! This thing just sprayed a goober all over me!"

The attendant spun around. "What are you doing in here? Animal enclosures are off-limits to visitors!" She yanked a walkie-talkie from her utility belt. "Security! This is Emma down with the camels. A boy with a huge nose just hopped the fence. Get here right away!"

Just then the spitting camel's bowels opened up and steamy clumps of brown dung balls plopped on the ground. The smell was unmistakable. The secret of Strange was inside the poop of a Bactrian camel!

CHAPTER 16

HUMPHREY

"I'm going to be a millionaire!" I snorted with glee.

"You're going to be arrested and fined," the zoo attendant growled at me. "Security is on the way."

I ignored her while my mental scent dictionary quickly broke down camel's waste product. There was a rich array of minerals, carbon, nitrogen, hydrogen, oxygen, and phosphorous. A few sniffs later, I had completely figured how Bactrian camel dung produced an intoxicating vanilla essence.

"Scientists first separate the chemicals in the dung and then process the different aromas at high heat and pressure. Presto! The end product is completely natural and an amazing alternative to synthetic vanillin!"

"What in the world are you mumbling about?" the zoo attendant said.

With the thrill of finally sniffing out the secret of Strange, I had totally forgotten that I had illegally entered the camel enclosure. My nostrils flared, hoping for a gust of wind to carry me to safety. There was nothing. The once-strong breeze was now a gentle whisper.

Three zoo security guards wearing badges and carrying nightsticks burst through a heavy metal door. The first guard was tall and skinny. The second one was short and plump, and the third guy looked like he was about eighty years old.

The zoo attendant pointed at me. "He's the one!"

I frantically searched my pockets for a bottle of cayenne pepper, hoping a little sniff could propel me back over the fence. Or at the very least, I could use it to give the guards a peppery sneeze while I made my escape. My heart sunk into my stomach. The only items I found were a half-eaten pack of

Sour Patch Kids and a palm full of sticky lint.

A loud grunting sound blasted in my ears. I turned around and saw the hairy Bactrian camel that had hockered on me. The thing was a huge male, standing at least seven feet tall. He calmly chewed on his cud while simultaneously spraying more loads of Strange-scented poop out of his butt. That's when the idea hit me. Without a second to lose, I leaped onto the camel and landed right between his two fuzzy humps.

"Giddy up!" I shouted, poking his ribs with my heels like I had seen cowboys do in the movies.

The camel didn't budge.

The tall guard burst out laughing. "That ain't no horsey, little boy."

"Camel rides start at noon on the main lawn," chimed in the plump one. "Get your tickets in the gift shop."

"Pictures included!" The old guy guffawed through a set of pearly white false teeth.

"Quit fooling around!" the zoo attendant ordered. "Get that kid off Humphrey before he gets hurt."

Humphrey must have been the camel's name.

What came next made me promise to give Humphrey a big, wet kiss after this was all over. As the three guards closed in on me, Humphrey's cheeks bulged like a giant prehistoric chipmunk. The camel then took aim and fired three rounds of gloppy, frothy spit right in their faces.

"Gross!" the plump guard cried.

"I just had my uniform dry cleaned, and now it's ruined!" shouted the old guy.

The zoo attendant grabbed a hunk of braided rope off the ground. She quickly tied it into a lasso. "Come off that camel this instant or I'll rope you like a suckling calf," she threatened.

"Open the gate, and I'll leave," I fired back. "No questions asked."

"You ain't going anywhere," the tall guard barked, his angry face still dripping with camel saliva. "You broke park rules. You're paying a hefty fine and then heading to juvie jail."

The word "jail" sent shivers down my nose. I could see the scenario play out in my head: Dr. Wackjöb paying my fine and then having to tell my parents that I was in juvie jail for breaking into a camel enclosure at the Central Park Zoo. After my prison stint, my parents would probably ground me for a year!

A loud Jeep painted to look like a tiger wheeled up to the camel exhibit. Two more security guards hopped out and made their way in my direction. As the Jeep sat idling, its exhaust backfired like a shotgun blast.

Humphrey went crazy.

With me still on his back, the camel stampeded through the enclosure. I grabbed a fistful of Humphrey's coarse hump hair and held on for dear life. We dashed past a bunch of Arabian camels munching on hay. They charged right along with us. Over a dozen crazed camels were now racing straight for the enclosure's wrought-iron fence. If Humphrey didn't put on the brakes soon, the collision was not going to be pretty.

I closed my eyes and awaited impact. At the last second, I felt Humphrey lurch to the left. And that's when I went flying off his back. Like a fighter pilot forced to use an ejection seat, I vaulted over the enclosure's fence and landed

nose first in front of a food cart selling Italian sausages.

"That was freaking awesome!" the guy behind the cart gushed. "I'll give you ten bucks to do it again."

"Offer me a million and then we'll talk," I said, wiping dirt off my honker.

"I'll give you sixty days in the slammer!" a familiar voice hollered from behind me.

I turned and saw the tall security guard, his pink face still glazed with camel spit. The guard pulled out a pair of handcuffs and lunged at me. I countered his attack by stabbing my nose hard into his belly. The guard cried out in pain, grabbed his stomach, and then crumbled to the ground.

The other guards rushed toward me. I kept them at bay by using my nose like a sword, slashing at them like an extra from a bad gladiator movie. Just as they were about to overtake me, Humphrey let out a loud grunt. He was staring at me through the fence with his big, sad camel eyes. He then turned around, pressed his butt pressed against the fence, and poured out globs of poop.

116

That was my cue.

I fought my way to the fence, scooped up two big fistfuls of Humphrey's million-dollar bum brownies, and sprinted as fast as I could back to the Boathouse.

CHAMEAU
MERDE

I was a wanted kid.

An ANB—All Nose Bulletin—went out for me. Every police officer assigned to Central Park was looking for me. Park-goers cleared out of my way as I hurried down the paths leading to the Boathouse. Swarms of flies, hungry for the clumps of poop in my hands, buzzed my head as I ran. After a close call with two of New York's finest, I finally arrived at the restaurant.

The hostess at the Boathouse refused to allow me inside.

"I told you," I pleaded with her. "I'm with

Pierre du Voleur. He rented a private room off the dining terrace."

"Leave here immediately before I call the police," the hostess said, holding her nose. "This is not a soup kitchen. You look and smell disgusting."

"I am not a homeless person! I am Pierre du Voleur's guest at this restaurant!"

"Let him in," a familiar French voice said from behind me.

I turned and saw Pierre. He was glaring at me, his temple vein throbbing and his face as red as a cherry-flavored Sour Patch Kid.

"But Mr. du Voleur—" the hostess protested.

"The boy is telling the truth," Pierre said. "He is my guest. Show him to the *toilette* so he can clean himself."

"Very well, sir," the hostess said and then reluctantly led me to the restroom.

I locked the door and stared at myself in the mirror. The hostess was right. I looked a mess. My nose was dirty; my jacket and jeans were ripped from flying head first out of the camel enclosure, and fresh hunks of camel dookie were dripping from my hands. However, I took offense at her telling me I smelled bad. What I carried in my hands was one of my most exciting fragrance discoveries since the Gates of Smell and Dr. Wackjöb's hákarl.

After carefully wrapping the camel poop in layers of paper towel, I scrubbed my nose and hands. My jacket and jeans still had big tears in them, but at least I wasn't dirty anymore. I opened the restroom door and saw Arnaud waiting for me.

"I hope for your sake, le Nez," Arnaud said ominously, "that whatever is wrapped inside that *serviette en papier* is what *Monsieur* du Voleur so desperately desires." He then grabbed me by the elbow and tugged me back to our private room.

"Give me one good reason why I shouldn't crush you like an *insecte* right now!" Pierre barked in my face.

"Because of this," I said, and then laid the poop wrapped in paper towels on the table.

"You filthy pig!" Pierre roared. "Get this *excrément* away from me!"

Arnaud attempted to grab the camel caca from the table, but I stopped him. "Don't touch it!" I hollered. "This is Bactrian camel dung. It's the secret of Strange! Jean Paul Puanteur uses it to make the subtle, vanilla-like scent that drives people crazy. But in a good way!"

"You have insulted *Monsieur* du Voleur for the last time," Arnaud said. "You will pay a heavy price for—"

Pierre raised his hand, cutting Arnaud off in mid-sentence. "Let le Nez speak. I want to hear more."

I told him everything. Running to the Central Park Zoo after I couldn't figure out the smell, illegally entering the camel enclosure, and finally figuring out that the Bactrian camel's backdoor bricks were the elusive last ingredient that made Strange the world's greatest perfume.

"I am confused," Pierre said, scratching his head. "How does Jean Paul turn common *chameau merde* into a powerful ingredient that smells like vanilla?"

"What's *chameau merde*?" I asked.

"Camel droppings," Arnaud answered.

"The main chemical compounds of camel poop are carbon, nitrogen, hydrogen, oxygen, phosphorous, and various other minerals," I explained. "Jean Paul must use a machine of some kind to separate the different chemicals."

"He most certainly uses a centrifugal separator," Pierre added.

I nodded. "You would know better than me. Anyway, he splits up the chemicals and then processes their different aromas at a very high heat with lots of pressure. What he ends up with is a natural, pleasing, and spectacular vanilla-like fragrance. The man's a genius. He actually created a brand-new smell!"

Pierre held his hands over his face in disbelief. "I should have known! Human beings have used various forms of *merde* to make fragrances for centuries. It was common from Roman times all the way to Napoléon III."

"Jean Paul claims he uses only natural ingredients for his fragrances," I said. "You can't get much more natural than good old-fashioned poop. I read a sign at the zoo that says the wild Bactrian camel is only found in Mongolia."

"This will be bigger than the fortune you made off of the Venezuelan bloated toad," Arnaud said. "I will call your private jet and put them on standby. We can assemble our men and fly to Mongolia immediately."

I was just about to ask what a toad had to do with anything when a Boathouse server entered the room. He carried a platter of food with one hand and a bottle of wine in the other.

"Just in time," I said. "I'm starving!"

I reached to grab a hunk of cheese and Pierre slapped my hand.

"Get away from my *déjeuner!*" he snapped. "Your work with me is *fini*, ended, over. Leave immediately."

"When will I get my million dollars?"

Arnaud laughed. "I don't remember you signing a contract for anything."

"But you told me I couldn't sign the contract until I figured out all the ingredients in Strange. Well, I figured it out, and now I'm ready to sign.

I want to be a *nez professionnel!*"

"You will never be a *nez professionnel*, and you will not receive payment," Pierre said coldly. "I told you to get out!"

I couldn't believe this was happening. A camel had nearly killed me and the cops had almost arrested me—all to get Pierre the secret ingredient. Now he was trying to cheat me out of my money!

"Not until you pay me!" I yelled.

"Call the police!" Pierre shouted to Arnaud.

Arnaud whipped out his cell phone. "Hello, 911? The boy wanted for causing a disturbance at the Central Park Zoo this morning is now attempting to rob patrons at the Boathouse restaurant on the lake. Please, hurry!"

"You're lying!" I cried. "You pulled the poop over my eyes and used my nose just to get the ingredient!"

Police sirens wailed in the distance. They were coming for me. I grabbed a fistful of cheese from the platter, angrily hurled the chunks at Pierre and Arnaud, and then fled the restaurant.

SUPER-VILLAIN

I was so furious that my nose spewed red-hot snot bubbles. How could I have been so stupid? Pierre du Voleur had just been using my gift of smell the whole time. All he wanted was the secret of Strange, and I'd handed it to him on a poopy paper towel filled with camel dung.

Jean Paul Puanteur was right.

Pierre was nothing but a thief and an untalented *insecte*.

Two New York City policemen on horseback galloped toward me. I dove into the bushes and watched them pass. They were heading straight for the Boathouse. Soon, the whole place was swarming with men in blue. The cops would bust me for sure if I didn't get out of the park right away.

A familiar scent drifted in the wind, and it wasn't Strange. Novelty fart spray from an aerosol can. Vivian, the Not-Right Brothers, and Dr. Wackjöb were signaling me! I leaped from my hiding place and dodged the police as I made my way down the busy New York streets. My nose followed the fake flatulence like a bloodhound. I sniffed over twenty blocks until I came to the same building where I had landed the gondola when we first arrived in New York.

After running up twenty flights of stairs, I pushed open the heavy metal door and stepped onto the roof. What I saw made my nostrils bug out of my nose.

"Jean Paul Puanteur," I said. "What are you doing here?"

The master perfumer, the legendary creator of Strange, was standing less than five yards from me. He was still wearing a black tuxedo with bright red Converse sneakers. Directly behind him were Vivian, the Not-Right Brothers, and Dr. Wackjöb.

Mumps shot a blast of fart spray into the air. "Nothing attracts Schnoz like a funky butt explosion," he said.

"Thank goodness you made it," Vivian said. "We were so worried about you."

"Way to get in trouble big time at the zoo," Jimmy joked. "You have the whole New York City Police Department looking for you."

A police helicopter buzzed overhead.

"Gríöarstór Nef, hide your nose!" Dr. Wackjöb shouted. "They have deployed helicopters in the search for your enormous proboscis!"

I dashed behind the water tower. The helicopter hovered over the building for a moment and then flew away, whining like a giant prehistoric mosquito.

"That was a close one," TJ said. "The news reports are saying that you tried to steal a camel in the zoo and then rob people in a restaurant."

"None of it's true," I said, stepping from behind the water tower.

"Of course it's not true," Vivian agreed. "You're a superhero, not a super-villain."

"There is only one super-villain," Jean Paul said bitterly. "And his name is Pierre du Voleur,"

I still couldn't believe Jean Paul was standing on the rooftop with the rest of the gang. "How... why...what?" I stuttered.

"Jean Paul came looking for us," Dr. Wackjöb said. "He got our names from the French restaurant last night."

"Pierre du Voleur is a notorious thief," Vivian said. "Jean Paul told us all about how he tries to steal more talented perfumer's creations."

"I researched it on the Internet," TJ added.

"Everything he says about Pierre du Voleur is true. The man's no good and rotten to the core."

TJ didn't have to tell me that. I already knew firsthand that Pierre was a lying dirty rat. And so was his weasel lackey, Arnaud.

"He is after your *nez*," Jean Paul said to me. "From what *Monsieur* Wackjöb says, you have the greatest *nez* and the most spectacular sense of *odeur* in the history of mankind."

"Schnoz can sniff out dog poop from over a hundred yards away!" Mumps chimed.

"And can sniff out minute fragrances as well," Jean Paul added. "Pierre wants nothing more than to steal my special ingredient in Strange. May I call you Schnoz?"

"You can call me anything but le Nez," I said. "That's what that rat Pierre calls me."

"Very well, Schnoz. If Voleur tries to trick you into revealing my ingredients, I implore you not to oblige him. It will not only ruin me, but destroy the livelihoods of many people around the world, as well as an endangered wild animal."

My heart dropped into my chest. I had done

something very bad and now felt like a pile of maggoty garbage. How could I tell Jean Paul that I had already revealed the secret of Strange to Pierre?

"I'm afraid this is my fault," Dr. Wackjöb said. "I knew Pierre du Voleur as a college student over thirty years ago. He contacted me a few days ago and invited us to New York as his guest. I'm the one who made the introduction."

"It's not your fault," Vivian said. "You had no idea your old college friend was a scumbag."

"She is right," Jean Paul added. "The only person at fault is Voleur. A man so devoid of morals that he tried to use a boy for his dirty work."

Jimmy slapped me on the back. "Well, thankfully my big-nosed friend here would never fall for something like that. Right, Schnoz?"

All eyes fell upon me. I quickly looked away.

"Right, Schnoz?" Jimmy repeated a little louder.

Jean Paul's face grew ashen. "You have been tricked into revealing the ingredient, haven't you?"

"Yes!" I cried out. "It's Bactrian camel poop! I'm sorry, but I didn't know Pierre was a fake!"

I rested my nose on Vivian's shoulder. A master

manipulator had fooled me, and I felt horrible. My insides felt like I had just swallowed a hunk of moldy tofu. I wanted to crawl inside my own nose and die.

"Stop feeling sorry for yourself, Schnoz," Vivian snapped at me. "You've been tricked by a sleazy criminal. It's happened to a lot of people. We need to focus our attention on what we can do *now*."

"What did you mean that uncovering the secret of Strange would destroy the livelihoods of people around the world and hurt endangered wild animals?" TJ asked.

A lump formed in Jean Paul's throat. His eyes grew watery; a single tear dripped down his cheek. "Gather around," he choked. "I will tell you the story of Camel Pee Shampoo."

CHAPTER 19

CAMEL PEE SHAMPOO

We all sat cross-legged on the black tar rooftop and listened to Jean Paul's tale of Camel Pee Shampoo.

"Many years ago when I was a *jeune homme* starting out in the *parfum et de la beauté* business," Jean Paul said, "I worked exclusively in hair care. Specifically, on how women could have fuller, thicker-looking hair, and how bald men could regrow the hair they had lost."

Jimmy patted Dr. Wackjöb's thinning scalp. "Listen closely. Maybe you can learn how to grow your hair back."

Dr. Wackjöb laughed. "Male pattern baldness is a sign of strength and virility!"

"Back then, my company sent me on a fact-finding mission," Jean Paul continued. "They wanted me to bring back to France the hair care secrets of Mongolian *femmes*. At the time, the women of the Gobi Desert were known to have the lushest, most beautiful hair in the world."

"Where are Mongolia and the Gobi Dessert?" Mumps asked.

"Mongolia is a country in northeast Asia bordering China in the south and Russia in the north," TJ answered. "The Gobi Desert covers parts of northern China and southern Mongolia. I didn't win the James F. Durante Geography Bee three years running with just my good looks."

Vivian rolled her eyes and then pressed a finger to her lips. "Shush. I want to hear this story."

The sound of a helicopter passing overhead caught everyone's attention. I quickly ducked behind the water tower and hid like before. Even though I hadn't done anything wrong (except enter the camel enclosure illegally), the New York

City police were pulling out all the stops trying to catch me. The helicopter buzzed the building for a couple minutes and then flew off. When the sky was clear, Jean Paul picked up his story.

"After landing in Ulaanbaatar, Mongolia's largest city, I became entranced by the culture and people," he said with a glint in his eye. "I hired a guide to take me deep into the desert. That's when I met a band of nomadic cattle herders and fell absolutely in *amour*."

"What's 'a…more' mean?" Mumps asked.

"Love," Vivian said. "Jean Paul fell in love."

TJ, Mumps, and Jimmy looked at each with the same *That's so gross* grimaces on their faces.

"In *amour* with a *femme* to be precise," Jean Paul mused. "Her name was Sarantstral, and she had the most beautiful, flowing, midnight black hair I had ever seen. With her stunning, exotic face, she could have easily been a *Vogue* cover model."

I raised my hand. "Sorry to interrupt, but what does a pretty Mongolian girl with nice hair have to do with camel pee?"

"You like to get to right to the point." He

chuckled. "I like that in a *homme*. As Sarantstral and I grew closer, she revealed to me the secret of her beautiful hair—the urine of the wild Bactrian camel native to the Gobi desert."

"Totally gross!" Jimmy chimed.

"Please don't tell us that your girlfriend washed her hair with camel pee!" TJ cried.

Mumps stood up and pointed to his skull. "See where the pigeon pooped on my head? It makes my hair all shiny. Maybe camel pee does the same thing."

"Not quite the same thing," Jean Paul offered. "But you are on the right track."

"Stop judging," Vivian barked at TJ and Jimmy. "Nomadic peoples have to make do with what they have."

"Boys, I had the same reaction when I saw Sarantstral wash her hair in camel urine for the first time," Jean Paul said. "I then realized that people all through the centuries have used urine to make soap, cleaning agents, and even toothpaste. She explained that only the urine of the *wild* Bactrian camel works for shampoo. Domesticated camel urine does not have the same shine and thickening properties as that of their wild cousins."

"Camel pee smells awesome!" I exclaimed. "Keep going!"

"To make a long story short, I brought home Sarantstral's secret of luxurious hair, and it set off a wave of *l' urine de chameau manie*—camel urine mania—in the European hair care industry."

Jean Paul then turned away, the expression on his face growing sad as painful memories flooded his brain. He wiped away a tear and finished the story. "Much like the American buffalo were almost brought to extinction for their hide, the wild Bactrian camels of the Gobi desert were exploited for their urine and are now nearly extinct—all because of me."

"What happened to Sarantstral?" Vivian asked.

"I do not know. The *urine de chameau manie* faded away rather quickly, and I never saw her again. The rush of foreign beauty companies racing into the desert for camel urine nearly destroyed their culture. Last I heard, she had fled with her family into the city slums to look for work."

No one said anything for the longest time. Vivian sniffled into a tissue, and the rest of us stared into space. Another helicopter passed overhead, but Jean Paul's tale of lost love was so depressing that I just let it pass without attempting to hide.

"I vowed to make it up to the people whose centuries-old way of life I had destroyed," Jean Paul said, his voice hoarse from emotion. "This is how I discovered that wild Bactrian camel dung, processed in the correct way, creates an elixir of *odeur* very similar to *vanille*."

"Why do you need *wild* camel dung?" I asked. "It would be easier to use poop from a zoo."

"Camels in the zoo eat dried hay and various grain pellets. Their wild brothers eat native Mongolian *herbes* and dry, thorny plants that other animals of the desert do not eat. Their natural diet makes the *différence*."

Jean Paul then explained that he pays bands of nomadic shepherds to follow the last wild herds of Bactrian camels of the Gobi Desert and collect their droppings. After collecting the camel's dung

137

humanely and without disturbing their natural habitat, they mail the sacks of dried poop to his laboratory in France for processing into Strange. They have a generous form of income, and Jean Paul has the main ingredient for a world-famous perfume.

"What will happen to the herdsman and camels now?" Jimmy asked.

"Pierre du Voleur is not a stupid man," Jean Paul explained. "He has no doubt brewed up a plan to hunt down and capture the last roaming wild camels. He will then cage them to make a cheap synthetic ingredient that imitates the smell of Strange. He has done this once before, when European cosmetic companies used the oily secretions of the Venezuelan bloated toad to make a wildly popular nail polish. The toad is now extinct—all because of Pierre du Voleur's greed."

I remembered Arnaud saying that Pierre had made a fortune off the Venezuelan bloated toad. How could anyone hunt a creature to extinction just for money? An image of Humphrey popped into my mind. I saw his sad camel eyes staring at me from behind the fence at the Central Park Zoo. His telepathic message to me was loud and clear. He had revealed the secret of Strange to me, and now I had to save his wild brothers and sisters in Mongolia.

"Everybody, head back to the hotel and grab your luggage!" I ordered. "We're checking out!"

"What are you talking about?" TJ wondered. "We still have four more days to see the New York sights."

I ran to the gondola and slipped on my Super Schnoz costume. My cape fluttered in the wind, while my Mardi Gras mask fit snugly and perfectly over my beak. "We're not staying in New York or even America for that matter," I said. "I'm flying us all to Mongolia so we can save the Bactrian camel!"

CHAPTER 20

SIX THOUSAND MILES

I rushed to the gondola and lifted the thick ropes around my shoulders.

"Hurry, everyone!" I hollered. "We're losing time!"

"Slow down, Schnoz," Vivian said. "This won't be like flying us from New Hampshire to New York. Mongolia is on the other side of the world!"

Vivian was right. Mongolia was thousands of miles away. Plus, the bulk of the flight would take place over a vast ocean. The trip would be dark and dangerous. My nostrils drooped in desperation. All I could think of were Pierre and

Arnaud slaughtering wild camels just to make loads of cash.

"Maybe we should take a commercial airline," Dr. Wackjöb suggested.

"No time," Jean Paul said. "There is not a direct flight from New York to Ulaanbaatar. It would take three days of changing planes to get there. And by that time, Voleur will have set his plan in *mouvement*."

"Pierre's already left for Mongolia," I said. "He has a private jet flying him there."

TJ flipped open his laptop and started googling. "New York to Mongolia—as the Schnoz flies—is roughly six thousand miles. For our Canadian and European friends, that's just over ten thousand kilometers."

"Impossible," Jimmy said. "We'll never make it."

"Nothing's impossible!" I cried. "I'm Super Schnoz, for sneezing out loud! I've crushed a lot stronger enemies than a sleazy French guy and his wormy little assistant. We have to find a way."

Everyone paced around the rooftop, trying to figure out how we could get to Mongolia before

Pierre commenced his camel genocide. TJ, Vivian, and Jimmy debated velocity and wind speeds. Dr. Wackjöb and Jean Paul discussed how they could get their hands on a Cessna Citation X, the fastest passenger plane in the world with a top speed over seven hundred miles an hour.

"What about Schnoz's solid rocket boogers?" Mumps suggested.

"What about them?" Jimmy grumbled.

"Just a few sniffs of cayenne pepper lifted us out of the backyard and all the way to New York City in a couple hours. Maybe if Schnoz snorted a bunch of pepper, he could fly a lot faster and farther."

"Mumps, you may be on to something," TJ said excitedly. "Let me crunch the numbers. This may take a while."

While TJ typed away on his laptop, Jimmy, Mumps, and Dr. Wackjöb hurried back to the hotel to collect our luggage. Jean Paul opened his wallet and showed Vivian and me a fading color photograph of Sarantstral. The woman was beautiful—long, black hair, pearly white teeth, and a perfectly round face. She was standing inside a large tent (Jean Paul called it a yurt), wearing a long purple tunic decorated with colorful beads and silver.

"She has a pair of Nike running shoes on her feet," Vivian noticed. "It really clashes with her traditional style of dress."

Jean Paul chuckled. "Yes, Sarantstral always had one foot firmly planted in tradition and the other reaching toward the future. I gave her those shoes as a gift for her nineteenth birthday."

"I got it!" TJ exclaimed. "I know exactly how we can get to Mongolia in less than twenty-four hours."

"Then let's hear it," Vivian said.

"Okay, put on your math caps and pay close attention. It took Schnoz six snorts of pepper to power us three hundred miles in two hours from New Hampshire to New York City. Mongolia is six thousand miles away. Six thousand divided by three hundred is twenty. Multiply twenty times two—meaning two hours—and that's how long it will take Schnoz to fly us to the capital city of Ulaanbaatar."

Jean Paul shook his head. "Forty hours is almost two days. We will be too late. Voleur has an *énorme* head start and will have already started his onslaught."

"Let me finish," TJ said impatiently. "Six snorts powered us for two hours. That's about an ounce of pepper. So, if Schnoz snorts two ounces of pepper every two hours instead of one, we can get there in twenty hours instead of forty. Get it?"

"Totally makes sense, TJ!" Vivian shouted. "That means Schnoz will need over eighty ounces of cayenne pepper for a round trip from America to Mongolia and back again. They sell those big sixteen-ounce jars at the Pepper Emporium. We can load up."

"Your *idée* just may work," Jean Paul said and then looked at me. "Do you think you can pull it off?"

I shook my nose. "It's a nice plan in theory, but it won't work in realty."

"What do you mean it won't work?" TJ asked, sounding a little miffed.

"My nose can't take that much heat. Do you

remember what happened when I battled ECU—Environmental Clean Up, the evil company that tried to close our school? Luckily, the battle with them ended before I bled to death from sniffing so much cayenne pepper. The stuff shredded my nasal lining!"

"Saline solution would do the trick," Vivian said. "But it would take a tanker truck full of water to keep your nose moistened enough to handle all of that hot pepper."

We all looked at the large, round water tower on top of the building. The same one I had hid behind when the police helicopters were prowling about.

TJ ascended the tower and peered inside. "It's full of water," he said. "My guesstimate is that it holds at least two hundred gallons."

"Will that be enough water?" Vivian asked me.

I shrugged. "Don't know, but we have to give it a try. The lives of endangered wild camels are at stake."

The water tower was way too heavy for us to lift by ourselves. TJ tied one end of the gondola's ropes to the water tower and then secured the other end around my shoulders. I took a snort of cayenne pepper, lifted the water tower in the air, and gently placed it inside the gondola.

"The tower takes up nearly the whole *gondole*," Jean Paul said.

Vivian climbed inside. "There's just enough room for all of us to fit reasonably comfortably," she observed. "But you can kiss our luggage good-bye. There's not enough room."

Just then, Jimmy, Mumps, and Dr. Wackjöb stepped onto the rooftop with our luggage. All three were red-faced and panting for breath.

"Thanks for getting the luggage," I said. "But we can't take it with us."

Jimmy's mouth dropped open. "Are you kidding me? The elevator's broken and we had to lug this stuff up twenty flights of stairs."

"Come with me, Mumps," Vivian said, zipping her jacket. "We're going shopping to stock up on cayenne pepper and food. We have a long trip ahead of us."

CRASH LANDING

TJ plotted our course on his laptop. I would fly eastward over the Atlantic Ocean, sailing through European and Russian airspace before finally landing in Mongolia. By his calculations, we should land in the capital city of Ulaanbaatar in just under nineteen hours. Jean Paul would then hire a guide to lead us into the desert after Pierre. I prayed that we had enough cayenne pepper and saline solution to get us there safely.

Everyone squeezed into the gondola. I took a snoot of pepper to ignite my solid rocket boogers and attempted to rise in the air. We didn't budge an inch. The tremendous weight of the water tower made liftoff nearly impossible.

"Take in more cayenne," Dr. Wackjöb suggested, tossing me a sixteen-ounce jar. "That should get us airborne."

I snorted up the fine red powder until my sniffer felt like it was on fire. After huffing nearly a half a bottle and letting out a mighty sneeze, I felt the gondola rising into the air and beginning its ascent over the city. Thankfully, TJ and Dr. Wackjöb had rigged a hose with a spray nozzle to the water tower. They drenched the insides of my burning honker with cool, refreshing H_2O.

Smooth sailing lasted only a few moments. When I had finally reached a comfortable altitude, a noisy helicopter buzzed my flank.

"This is the New York State Division of Homeland Security!" a loudspeaker rang out over the whine of helicopter wings. "Identify yourself immediately!"

"*Holy schnozola!*" I hollered down to the gang. "First, police whirlybirds are hunting me down for something I didn't do, and now the government is nipping at my nose!"

"They must think we are *terroristes*," I heard Jean Paul say.

"What are you going to do?" Vivian shouted.

"I'm going to do what they want and identify myself!" I said.

I closed one nostril with my finger and banked hard to the right. The helicopter was now directly in front of me. We starred at each other like a turkey buzzard and bald eagle squaring off over an animal carcass. Two uniformed men were inside. One flew the chopper; the other clutched a high-powered rifle.

"Identify yourself!" the pilot repeated through the loudspeaker.

"I'm Super Schnoz!" I yelled and then inhaled another snoot full of pepper. The blistering sneeze that followed was so powerful it propelled me away from the helicopter and over Long Island Sound. The skyscrapers of Manhattan slowly faded away in the distance. The waters of the Atlantic Ocean lay below like a giant green carpet. Mumps turned on the hose and gave my hard-working honker a well-deserved nasal flush, and we were on our way to save the Bactrian camel.

Four hours and two jars of cayenne pepper later, the European continent came into view.

"Land ho!" Jimmy shouted. "We made it!"

"We haven't made it anywhere," I heard TJ say. "We still have a good fifteen hours of flying left before we land in Mongolia."

"My sinuses need another blast of water!" I yelled from up above. "I feel a bloody nose coming on."

Jean Paul grabbed the hose and fired a round of warm water into my dried mucous membranes. The relief was instantaneous. Without the water, the trip would not be possible.

"Thanks," I said. "Now, toss me up one of those chocolate protein bars. I'm starving."

Night fell as we passed over Paris. Below my feet, the Eiffel Tower looked like a bright Christmas tree. While Jean Paul entertained Vivian and the Not-Right Brothers with stories about his native city, I focused on the stars. The alien Apneans, who just a few months earlier had collected my snores to take over the world, were up there somewhere. I wondered if they had found another planet to take over. Or were they planning another invasion of Earth?

Hundreds of miles later, the lights of Europe's major cities gave way to utter blackness. TJ had calculated we were somewhere in the middle of Siberia. Exhaustion tugged at my flapping nostrils. I desperately wanted to land in some desolate patch of woods and rest, but every lost second meant the life of an endangered camel. I caught a gust of wind, inhaled more pepper, and kept sniffing along.

Finally, as I neared my nineteenth hour of continuous flying, we crossed over the Russian border into Mongolia. The gang let out a loud *whoop*, but the grueling trip had fried my nose so badly that I couldn't show any emotion. The first rays of morning sun peeked over the horizon. Below us, the Gobi Desert stretched as far as the eye could see. The landscape was harsh, barren, and completely void of life.

"Are you sure we didn't blow off course and land on Mars?" Jimmy joked.

"The Gobi is rocky with very sparse vegetation," Jean Paul explained. "Unlike deserts we are all used to seeing, there are very few sand dunes. The harsh terrain discourages human habitation except for *rubuste* souls."

"Like Sarantstral and her fellow desert dwellers?" Vivian asked.

Jean Paul nodded. "Yes. She came from very *résilient* stock. Also, the Gobi is known for *extrêmement* violent and unpredictable dust storms with very high wind…"

Before Jean Paul could finish his sentence, a huge, tornado-like dust cloud appeared out of nowhere. A blast of yellow sand blew directly in my face. Dirt and debris clogged my nose, causing my nostrils to deflate. The ropes over my shoulders that I used to carry the gondola twisted up like a kindergartner's shoestrings. The water tower tipped over, dumping gallons of water and nearly crushing TJ and Dr. Wackjöb under its weight. We then went into a deadly tailspin and plunged toward the desert floor.

"Throw me some pepper so I can keep us from crashing!" I yelled.

Mumps dove for the last jar of cayenne that was rolling around inside the gondola. Just as he wrapped his fingers around it, another fierce blast of wind whipped us sideways. The jar popped out of his hand and disappeared over the side.

"It's gone!" Mumps cried out. "We're going to die!"

I shoved two fingers deep inside my nose, desperately trying to scrape my nostrils free of sand so I could get some wind. It was useless. The more sand I picked from my snout, the more that came flying right back in.

Vivian, the Not-Right Brothers, Dr. Wackjöb, and Jean Paul grabbed hands, praying for their lives. I tilted my nose down, closed my eyes, and awaited impact.

CHAPTER 22

MY KINGDOM FOR A HORSE

An image of Jimmy's black cat, Igor, flashed in my mind as I plummeted to the ground. One afternoon we were all hanging out inside the Nostril when Vivian noticed Igor on top of Jimmy's roof. The cat had climbed from an attic window to stalk a flock of pigeons roosting near the chimney. What happened next was the most amazing feat of aerial acrobatics I had ever seen.

A stray pigeon wandered within Igor's striking distance. The cat pounced from his hiding spot, but instead of getting the pigeon, he accidentally leaped off the rooftop. I remember watching in amazement as Igor twisted in midair like an Olympic diver until all four of his paws were squarely under his body. He landed with a *thump* in a patch of mulch. I thought for sure the cat was dead or badly hurt. But he just gave his body a quick shake and then trotted back inside the house.

If we were to survive this fall, I would have to perform the same daredevil act as Igor.

The cat had used his tail and flexible backbone to right himself. I, on the other hand, needed to use my bendy booger beak. Everyone has a tiny nasalis muscle whose sole function is to flare the nostrils. The difference between my nasalis and one of a normal person is like the Thing and a little old lady flexing biceps. There is no comparison.

I squeezed my nasalis muscle with all my might. Slowly, the mass of fleshy cartilage in the center of my face started wiggling. My mutated mucous monster jiggled faster. The dirt and sand clogging up my snot sewer began falling away. I was getting air! Just before we crashed, the external openings of my nasal cavity inflated like a stuntman's air bag. Vivian, the Not-Right Brothers, Dr. Wackjöb, and Jean Paul crashed on top of me, my bouncy nose breaking their fall.

"Is anyone hurt?" I asked, panting for breath.

"*Owww!*" Mumps cried out in pain. "My ankle!"

The gang jumped off my muzzle and rushed to help Mumps.

"Careful," Vivian warned. "He may have a broken bone."

Dr. Wackjöb gently rolled up Mumps's pant leg. "It's bruising already," he said. "Can you move it?"

Mumps gritted his teeth. After a moment, his foot moved a couple millimeters.

"If you can move it, then it's not broken," Dr. Wackjöb said. "It looks to me like a very bad sprain. You just need some R-I-C-E."

"I'm not hungry," Mumps groaned, still obviously in pain.

"RICE is an acronym that means rest, ice, compression, elevation," Vivian said. "My grampy's an emergency-room nurse."

"Rest, compression, and elevation we can do," Jimmy said. "But where do you expect to find ice? We just crashed in the middle of a dry desert!"

Everyone stopped what they were doing and gazed at the vast horizon. As far as the eye could see, there was nothing but a foreign landscape of rocks, pebbles, boulders, and dirt.

"What do we do now?" I groaned. "We're out of food and water."

"Plus, my laptop was completely destroyed in the fall," TJ added, salvaging the computer's hard drive.

Jean Paul climbed a small, rocky hill and surveyed the surroundings. "This is the landscape of northern Mongolia," he said. "If TJ's calculations were correct and we crossed over the border between Russia and Mongolia, then Ulaanbaatar is somewhere south of here. Schnoz, can you fly there to find us help?"

I lifted my nose in the air. Only a moment ago a wicked windstorm had been blowing dirt and sand everywhere. Now, the air was still without even the slightest breeze.

"Not without wind or cayenne pepper," I said. "Until Mother Nature decides to whip up a gust, I walk like everyone else."

Vivian tore a hunk of fabric from her jacket and wrapped Mumps's injured ankle. TJ and Jimmy helped him climb onto Dr. Wackjöb's back.

"Mumps cannot put any pressure on his ankle or it will never heal," Dr. Wackjöb said. "I will take the first shift carrying him. Fortunately, my young friend is a pipsqueak and doesn't weigh much."

Using the rising sun as our guide, we walked south toward Ulaanbaatar. By nine a.m., the air was already dry and hot. By the time noon rolled around, the temperature was scorching. We all huddled against a big boulder that offered a minuscule amount of shade.

"Water," Vivian said. Her voice was weak and her lips chapped from sun exposure. "I'll give my kingdom for a glass of water."

"That is from a Shakespeare play," Dr. Wackjöb said and then lifted Mumps off his back. "*Richard III*, I believe. But the line is 'My kingdom for a horse,' not water."

"I'd rather have water right now instead of a horse," I said, trying to shield my already sunburned nose.

Jean Paul abruptly stood up. "Look in the distance," he said. "Do you see that kick-up of *poussière?*"

I assumed that *poussière* meant dust, because that is exactly what I saw on the horizon. It wasn't huge like the dust storm that had crashed the gondola, but several small dust devils whirling like spinning tops.

"I hear hoofbeats!" Jimmy cried out. "They're horses!"

"You are correct," Jean Paul said. "Men are riding them—at least a dozen—and they are coming this way!"

The only thing I could think of was Genghis Khan and the Mongol horde. Were these men going to rob us and leave us for dead in this forsaken desert? Before we had time to react, the horses had reached us.

The riders wore long, elaborately decorated robes with hoods that concealed their faces. Long swords, sharp knives, and bows with quivers dangled from their mounts. They shouted at us in a foreign language I assumed to be Mongolian.

159

The rider in front, obviously the leader, drew his sword, hopped off his horse, and approached us. I thrust out my nose, ready to defend my friends. The sudden appearance of my menacing honker took the man by surprise. He took a step back and yanked off the hood hiding his face. That's when I realized that he was really a *she*. The other riders yanked off their hoods as well.

They were all women!

FLYING DRAGON NOSE

The woman standing before me looked slightly different from the others. She was young, with long, black hair and intense dark eyes, but her face was angular and not as round as the rest of the women. Under her robe, she wore what I assumed to be a traditional Mongolian outfit—except for her shoes. On her feet was a brand-new pair of red Converse sneakers, just like Jean Paul was wearing.

Jean Paul stepped forward and took one look at the woman, and his mouth dropped open in shock. "Sarantstral," he blubbered. "Is it really you? You haven't changed one bit in *trente* years!"

The woman clutched her sword. "I was not even alive thirty years ago," she said. "And why do you call me by my mother's name?"

Her perfect English and the fact that she knew the word *trente* meant "thirty" in French surprised me. The other women slid off their horses. They huddled around their leader with weapons drawn.

"I will ask you again," she said. "How do you know my mother's name?"

Jean Paul stared at her deeply, his eyes carefully studying her face. As he reached out to touch her, the woman grabbed his arm and flung him to the ground like a wet towel. The other horsewomen rushed toward us, ready to fight if we made any sudden moves.

"He was in love with a Mongolian girl named Sarantstral a long time ago," Vivian said, trying to diffuse the situation. "You must have reminded him of her. That's all. We've flown here from the United States and crashed in the desert. A very bad man wants to capture a bunch of wild Bactrian camels, and we need to stop him."

A shocked expression washed over the woman's face. She turned to her fellow horsewomen, jabbered something in Mongolian, and then faced us.

"I don't believe you," the woman said angrily "You are with the Frenchman and his foreign fighters. You have invaded our villages and forced our husbands and brothers to help you search for our sacred camels. You want them all!"

"We don't want to take camels," I said. "We want to *save* them. The Frenchman you're talking about wants the camels to make an ingredient for his horrible perfume."

"Just like when my mother was young, when foreigners invaded the desert to collect camel urine for shampoo."

One of the horsewomen gave me a sinister look. She raised her sword in the air, seconds from be-nosing me, chopping my cookie detector right off my face. That's when Jean Paul struggled to his feet, reached into his pocket, and pulled out the fading photograph of Sarantstral wearing the purple tunic and Nike running shoes.

"Her name is Sarantstral," Jean Paul said, handing the photo to the head horsewoman. "We once loved each other."

The woman studied the photo, looked up at Jean Paul, and then stared back at the photo. "This is my mother as a young woman," she said. "And you…you…" The words became stuck in her throat. She took a deep breath. "You must be Jean Paul…my father."

Jean Paul and the woman collapsed into each other's arms, tears flowing down their cheeks.

"What is your name?" Jean Paul asked his newly discovered daughter.

"Bayarma Juliette," she answered. "My mother wanted me to have a Mongolian first name and a French second name in honor of my father."

"Where is Sarantstral now? I must know."

Before Bayarma answered, the sounds of gunfire blasted in the distance.

"Sorry to interrupt the father and daughter reunion," I said. "But we came here on a mission. We need to think of a way to save those camels!"

Bayarma composed herself and then clustered with her crew. The horsewomen debated loudly back and forth with each other.

"What are they shouting about?" Jimmy wondered.

"Something about how they are *considérablement* outnumbered," Jean Paul said. "It's been a long time since I've heard anyone speak the Mongolian language, but I can make out a few words here and there."

Bayarma turned to us. "I am sorry to say that our cause is lost. The Frenchman…"

"The rat's name is Pierre," TJ interjected.

"The Frenchman, Pierre, has at least one hundred heavily armed men. They are not Mongolians, but from different European countries."

"He employs *criminels* from Germany, Spain, France, Austria, and even the United States," Jean Paul said. "I saw their destruction firsthand in Venezuela when they hunted the bloated toad to extinction."

A rush of wind whipped through the dry desert valley. I braced myself for another dust storm, but the breeze was clear of any dirt and debris. I inhaled a big gust, and my nostrils inflated to the size of a camping tent. My toes dangled above the ground. I let out a big snort and rose about twenty feet in the air.

The horsewomen took one look at me hovering in midair and ran to their horses like a herd of frightened sheep.

"*Luu khamar nisdeg…luu khamar nisdeg!*" they shouted in Mongolian.

"What are they saying?" Vivian asked.

"Flying dragon nose," Bayarma answered. "They think he has the powerful nose of a flying dragon."

Mumps lifted his head and snickered through the ankle pain. "Give him some cayenne pepper, and Schnoz will be a flying dragon nose who breathes fire."

"Schnoz, come back down!" Vivian shouted to me. "You're freaking these ladies out."

I closed one nostril and drifted to the ground. "It feels so good to fly," I said. "The wind is pretty strong right now. I can do a reconnaissance flight and see if I can locate Pierre and his men."

"That won't do any good," Jimmy said.

"Sure it will," Dr. Wackjöb countered.

"No it won't. You heard what Bayarma said. Pierre has over a hundred men experienced in killing! They're probably carrying M4 carbines, MK13 grenade launchers, AR15 assault rifles, and a bunch of other military-style guns. We have six unarmed people, one of who is injured, and twelve tough women armed with swords, knives, and bows. I'd say the odds are pretty much against us."

"But they don't have a flying dragon nose!"

Mumps shouted.

Everyone looked at me. For the first time since becoming Super Schnoz, I didn't feel like a super-hero. My dirty, shredded Super Schnoz costume hung off me in threads. The Mardi Gras mask disguising my nose was long gone.

"Jimmy's right," I said, hanging my nose in shame. "I can still fly, but without any pepper to fuel my cayenne canyon, we'll never defeat Pierre and save the camels."

"What do you need pepper for?" Bayarma asked. "And what is this 'cayenne cannon' you are talking about?"

Vivian, the Not-Right Brothers, and Dr. Wackjöb spent the next five minutes explaining how I had crushed ECU and the Apneans just by using the power of my nose and a snuffler full of spicy pepper.

Bayarma's eyes grew wide with excitement. "You are coming with us," she said, jumping on her horse. "If his big *khamar* just needs hot pepper to blow up army tanks and defeat aliens, then I may have exactly what you're looking for."

CHAPTER 24

DANCE OF THE BUDDHA

The women helped us onto their horses, and we galloped across the desert. Thankfully, they had lots of water for us to drink. I wanted to inflate my nostrils and fly, but Bayarma asked me to share her horse, a fleet Mongolian stallion she called Od, which she told me meant Star in her native language.

"How do you speak English so well?" I asked as we scurried up a rocky embankment.

"I am fluent in Mongolian, English, French, Russian, Mandarin Chinese, and the slang of American hip-hop," she answered. "I was raised herding cattle in the Gobi, but I graduated from Inner Mongolia University with a degree in foreign languages."

"What about the other women? Do they speak English as well?"

Bayarma shook her head. "No. They have lived their entire lives as nomadic Gobi herders."

We rode in silence for a long time. The only sounds were pounding horse hooves and blowing gusts of wind. A plume of black smoke rose from a camp in the distance. Bayarma let out a cry of despair, slapped her horse, and raced toward the camp like she was in the home stretch of the Kentucky Derby.

When we got there, the scene was one of utter destruction. Several yurts were ablaze, all of the animals were gone. Bayarma hopped off Od, clutched her sword, and examined the carnage.

"Mother, Grandmother!" she screamed at the top of her lungs. "*Eej ni, Emee,* where are you?"

The other horsewomen frantically joined in the search for friends and loved ones, but there was no one. The place was completely empty of people.

"The Frenchman and his brutes have raided the

camp and taken more of our mothers, grandmothers, and sisters to help find the camels!" Bayarma said, her face flaming with fury. "If we don't find them quickly, who knows what will happen!"

Vivian slid off her horse and ran up to me. "Schnoz, you're the only person who can help. We need to come up with a plan and fast."

She was right. I didn't fly us across the world just to watch yurts burn. I walked up to Bayarma, grabbed her shoulders, and shouted, "Keep calm and smell on! We all need to have clear heads. You said something about pepper. Tell me more."

Vivian, the Not-Right Brothers, Dr. Wackjöb, Jean Paul, Bayarma, and I powwowed around an overturned cooking pot. The tension and desperation in the air was so thick I could sniff it with a spoon.

Bayarma grabbed a cloth sack full of dried peppers about the size of a finger. "The pepper is called bird's eye chili," she explained. "We use it in many Mongolian dishes."

Vivian, Jimmy, and Bayarma each grabbed a handful of the peppers and then pulverized them to dust with a stone pestle and mortar. I quickly snorted up a wad, aimed my nose at a rocky mound, and let out a sneeze. The peppery blast that followed made my nose hairs dangle in defeat. Instead of blasting the rock to smithereens, the sneeze merely made two watermelon-sized indentions in its side.

"The pepper's not powerful enough," I whined.

While I lamented about my weak, wimpy sneeze, Dr. Wackjöb grabbed a handful of the crushed peppers and examined them closely.

"We just need to enhance the capsaicin," Dr. Wackjöb muttered.

TJ scratched his head. "What's capsaicin?"

"Capsaicin is the main chemical compound that makes peppers hot," Dr. Wackjöb explained. "If only I had some *allyl isothiocyanate* to increase the naturally occurring capsaicin production."

"Where do you get 'all…ill…iso…thio… whatever'?" I asked.

"Allyl isothiocyanate is the oil responsible for the hot taste of horseradish and wasabi."

Bayarma produced another sack and handed it

to Dr. Wackjöb. "Do you mean this?"

Dr. Wackjöb opened the bag and took a whiff. His cheeks turned red and his eyes started watering. "This is the most powerful horseradish root I have ever seen," he said, fanning his face from the heat. "Where do you get it?"

"It grows wild in certain areas of the Gobi," Bayarma said.

"TJ, grab the pestle and mortar," Dr. Wackjöb ordered. "You and I are going to try to make the most powerful pepper mutation known to man."

Three of Bayarma's horsewomen approached me. They bowed politely and then tossed a bundle of colorful fabric at my feet.

"What's this stuff?" I asked.

"It's a costume from one of our *Tsam* dances," Bayarma said. "*Tsam* means 'dance of the Buddha.'" She rummaged through the fabric and yanked out the most awesome, freaky, scary mask I had ever seen.

"It's a dragon mask!" Jimmy exclaimed. "Try everything on."

The mask was fiery red with huge golden eyes and pearly white fangs. Bright yellow feathers

finished off the presentation. I carefully slipped the mask over my head. The dragon's papier-mâché snout fit perfectly over my massive beak. I then slipped into the rest of the costume.

Bayarma smiled. "Wonderful! You look like a Mongolian *Tsam* dancer."

A hard squall blew through the camp. My nasal cavity inhaled the breeze, expanding my nostrils. I drifted steadily into the air. The dragon costume's red tail flapped in the wind.

"I'm off to scout for Pierre!" I yelled from up above. "When I find him, I'll be back, and we can start our assault. Hopefully, Dr. Wackjöb and TJ will have the pepper ready for me to blast them into the Stone Age."

I sucked in a deep snoot full of air, pointed my honker toward the horizon, and flew off into the clouds.

174

CHAPTER 25

BATTLE OF THE BACTRIANS

After thirty minutes in the air, I finally sniffed out Pierre and his soldiers. They were in a dry desert valley, pursuing a panicked herd of wild Bactrian camels that were for the moment just out of firing range.

I sailed high above them, scoping out their operation. Jimmy's hunch had been correct; the militia carried powerful rifles and machine guns, and drove military-style jeeps and Hummers. Trudging behind the squadron were at least two dozen frightened Mongolian men, women, children. Thick ropes bound them together while four of Pierre's goons forced them to march.

"Bayarma's people," I said aloud. "I bet her mother, Sarantstral, is one of them."

As I banked left to turn my beak around and return to the gang, a round of gunfire blasted over my head, barely missing my nose. I looked down and saw a bunch of Pierre's men firing at me.

"What kind of ugly bird is that?" one of the men shouted.

"Looks like a big kite shaped like a dragon," said another.

"Let's shoot that sucker out of the sky!" cried a third man.

A bullet clipped the end of my dragon's tail, sending a spray of yellow feathers and papier-mâché into the air. I sniffed harder, quickly flying out of firing range, and headed back to my friends.

Everyone was waiting for me when I finally landed. A million questions flew in my direction.

"Did you find them?"

"How many are there?"

"What about their guns and equipment?"

Bayarma rushed up to me. "Did you see my mother?"

"Maybe," I answered. "They were forcing a couple dozen of your people to march with them. One of them was probably your mother."

Dr. Wackjöb and TJ emerged from over the ravine carrying a large clay pot.

"Does the pepper work?" I asked.

"We don't know," Dr. Wackjöb said. "You have to test it out first."

I looked into the pot expecting to see a bunch of ground pepper. Instead, I saw a bunch of little brown balls the size of Milk Duds.

"What's this stuff?" I asked, scratching the end of my nose.

"Simply grinding both peppers and mixing them together did not change the levels of cap-saicin," Dr. Wackjöb explained. "TJ and I had to boil each of the ingredients down to this clay-like substance. We're hoping that heating the combined properties of the bird's eye chilis and the Mongolian horseradish root will greatly increase its heat."

I grabbed two of the pepper balls and shoved one up each nostril. The sting was so intense

I nearly passed out. My elephant trunk started tickling. I aimed my nose at a rocky mound and sneezed. The boogery blast that shot from my cayenne cannon sounded like a howitzer going off. My brain throbbed and my ears rang. The pepper balls, combined with my atomic snot, exploded the mound to pieces and left a crater the size of a Florida sinkhole.

"Success!" Dr. Wackjöb and TJ cheered, slapping each other a high five.

We finalized our battle plan. Vivian, Bayarma, and I would fly ahead to bombard Pierre and his men with pepper balls. The rest of the gang would ride on horseback with the women to guard my flank.

We all bent over until our noses were touching.

"On the count of three," I said. "One, two, three…"

"SUPER SCHNOZ!" we all screamed.

Vivian and Bayarma strapped the clay pot filled with pepper balls on my back and climbed on board, and we soared into the clouds. As we approached Pierre's men, I saw my worst nightmare was coming true. They had found the herd of Bactrian camels and were now rounding them up.

"Ammo!" I ordered. "Quickly!"

Vivian and Bayarma shoved a round of pepper balls up my nostrils. I swooped low and fired on a group of men. They had just lassoed an adult camel and two nursing calves. My aim was perfect. The pepper balls made a direct hit, and the camels escaped over a hill and out of sight.

The Battle of the Bactrians had begun.

Pierre's men were everywhere, rounding up the innocent camels. I swooped and dove like an animated dragon in a Disney movie, blowing away the camel rustlers with my pinpoint, pepper-ball-fueled booger blasts.

Pierre and Arnaud came into view. They were riding in an open-air Hummer, pointing into the sky, and ordering the men to stop hunting camels and start shooting at me. Dozens of men trained their sights in my direction.

"I need more pepper balls!" I shouted to Vivian and Bayarma.

I felt Vivian's hand reach around my head and

shove a single pepper ball up my honker.

"It's the last one," she said dejectedly.

"At least we will have died trying to save innocent camels," Bayarma said.

I saw a cloud of dust appear on the horizon. The horsewomen stormed onto the battlefield carrying the Not-Right Brothers, Dr. Wackjöb, and Jean Paul. TJ and Mumps hopped off the horses and hurled globs of fresh camel poop at Pierre's men. The fleeing camels suddenly turned on the men, spitting wads of slobbery goop into their eyes. Before the thieves could wipe the poop and spit from their faces, Vivian, Dr. Wackjöb, and Jean Paul had freed the captured Mongolians.

Half of Pierre's men raced after their former captives, the other half fired at me. A bullet clipped the dragon mask, causing it to fly off my head. The gunfire missed my flesh, but the impact knocked me sideways. Before I could right myself, I was dive-bombing directly toward Pierre's Hummer.

"This can't be!" I heard Pierre cry. "It's…it's le Nez! You are destroying all my plans!"

"I've been saving this for you two!" I sneered

and then sneezed the final pepper bomb at the two evil perfumers. The explosion split the Hummer in two. Pierre and Arnaud stumbled from the burning vehicle and attempted to flee, but Dr. Wackjöb and a horsewoman quickly wrestled them to the ground.

"Hello, old friend," Dr. Wackjöb growled in Pierre's face. "I will greatly enjoy turning you over to the Mongolian authorities."

I turned to check on the others. What I saw blew my nose with joy. Using only swords, knives, and bows and arrows, the horsewomen had chased down the rest of Pierre's men and quickly subdued them.

When the dust settled, I saw Bayarma and Jean Paul hugging a beautiful older woman with streaks of gray in her Halloween-black hair. The woman was wearing a worn pair of Nike running shoes.

Jean Paul had finally found Sarantstral.

A GIFT OF CAMEL

After three days of traveling, we landed in New York and then took a quick commuter flight back to New Hampshire. Dr. Wackjöb had booked us a first-class flight out of Mongolia. Thank goodness, because the thought of flying six thousand miles back to the United States with nose power made my sinuses want to explode.

My spent honker needed a well-deserved vacation.

The smell of Strange was still everywhere, and I kept thinking about Jean Paul. He had decided to stay in Mongolia to be with Bayarma and Sarantstral.

When I made it back home, I gave each of my parents a gift from the trip. Instead of picking them up an I LOVE NEW YORK T-shirt or an Empire State Building key chain, I got them each a traditional Mongolian hat that I had picked up at a shop inside the Ulaanbaatar airport. I told them all about visit to the Big Apple, except for my experiences with Pierre and Arnaud and the New York City Police Department. I also left out that little part about flying six thousand miles to the Gobi Desert and fighting evil camel poachers.

Two months later, Dr. Wackjöb invited Vivian, the Not-Right Brothers, and me to his office for lunch. The weather was too cold to ride bikes, so Vivian's mom dropped us off. When we walked into his office, Jean Paul and Bayarma were standing there.

We all gave them a big hug.

"What are you two doing here?" I asked.

"I thought you stayed in Mongolia," TJ said.

"Where's Sarantstral?" Jimmy wondered.

Jean Paul chuckled. "One question at a time. First, Bayarma and I are here because we wanted to say *merci* for everything you did for us."

"Second, I am now in a master's program at Columbia University in New York," Bayarma said. "I'm studying conservation biology with a specialization in the wild Bactrian camel."

"And third," Dr. Wackjöb added, "I invited Sarantstral to come, but she is too vital in the lives of her people to leave the Gobi Desert."

We spent the next hour eating pizza and reminiscing about our time in Mongolia. Jean Paul informed us that Pierre and Arnaud were now serving a five-year sentence in one of Mongolia's toughest prisons for entering the country illegally with instruments of war.

Then Jean Paul turned to me and said, "Bayarma and I have something to show you."

Dr. Wackjöb led us through the Gecko Glue® and Snore Cure Mist® factory and outside into the back parking lot. Five inches of snow had fallen overnight, blanketing everything in white. We stopped in front of a flatbed truck loaded with a huge metal crate.

Jean Paul handed me a key. "Unlock the crate. Inside is a *présent* for you."

I gave Vivian and the Not-Right Brothers a confused look and slipped the key into the lock. When I opened the crate, my nose nearly fell off.

"Humphrey!" I exclaimed.

The camel trotted out of the crate and nuzzled his hairy face against my nose.

"This is the camel I told you about," I said to Vivian and the Not-Right Brothers. "He's from the Central Park Zoo."

"So this is the camel that finally gave you the secret of Strange," Jimmy said.

"You mean its poop gave up the secret." Mumps chortled.

"And don't forget," TJ added, "this thing almost got you arrested by the New York City police!"

"Why…how…" I stammered.

"The Central Park Zoo is closing its camel exhibit," Bayarma explained. "Other zoos offered to take the Arabian camels, but there were no takers for the lone Bactrian."

"I made a sizeable donation to the zoo and assumed responsibly for the camel," Jean Paul said.

Bayarma explained that she had wanted to ship

Humphrey to Mongolia to be with his wild brothers. However, after talking with a zoo official, she decided that it would be extremely difficult—if not impossible—to return a habituated animal to its wild state.

"I have purchased thirty acres of cleared woodland outside town," Dr. Wackjöb said. "That will be Humphrey's new home. I assume that you five will take responsibility for his care and feeding."

I was so happy that I wrapped my arms around Humphrey's neck. The camel licked my nostrils, puffed up his cheeks, and then fired a wad of spit right in my face. A camel saliva bath had never felt so good.